ad

DEC 1 2 2012

DATE DUE			

OTHER WORKS BY JOHN TOOMEY

Sleepwalker

Huddleston Road

JOHN TOOMEY

DALKEY ARCHIVE PRESS
CHAMPAIGN • DUBLIN • LONDON

Library of Congress Cataloging-in-Publication Data
>
> Toomey, John, 1975-
> Huddleston Road / John Toomey. -- 1st ed.
>   p. cm.
> ISBN 978-1-56478-781-1 (pbk. : alk. paper) -- ISBN 978-1-56478-
812-2
> (cloth : alk. paper)
> 1. Unmarried couples--Fiction. 2. Love-hate relationships--Fiction.
3.
> London (England)--Fiction. 4. Psychological fiction. I. Title.
> PR6120.O56H83 2012
> 823'.92--dc22
>   2012021661
>

Partially funded by a grant from the Illinois Arts Council, a state agency

www.dalkeyarchive.com

Printed on permanent/durable acid-free paper and bound in the United
States of America

Huddleston Road

To Brendan and Margaret, Dad and Mam,
For boundless love and lessons in compassion

Acknowledgements

The beginnings of *Huddleston Road* go a long way back, but once the decision to impose a novel upon the idea was made, a number of writers and sources became influential in its realization. I was struggling to find a coherent narrative when I came across Victoria Gill's excellent article, *Suicide Surfers*, in the *Sunday Times Magazine* in May 2007. The article alerted me to the internet suicide phenomena, A.S.H., which I would go on to adapt for my own purposes in the form of DUST. I borrowed liberally from the A.S.H. site, now frozen for posterity, embellishing and adapting it to suit the narrative of *Huddleston Road*.

I would also like to thank John Waters, writer and journalist with *The Irish Times*, for his kind appraisal of my first novel, *Sleepwalker*, and his subsequent help with the recommended reading for *Huddleston Road*. The book certainly could not have been written without Al Alvarez's deeply personal insight into suicide and its place in literature through the ages, in his superb book, *The Savage God*. Mr Alvarez imposed humanity on the cultural history of suicide, made accessible the ideas and theories without ever losing sight of their labyrinthine complexity.

On the advice of John Waters, I also dipped in and out of Emile Durkheim's sociological tome, *Suicide,* which was invaluable, and Primo Levi's, *The Drowned and the Saved*, which must be one of the bravest pieces of writing I've encountered.

I should mention, too, that the internet and its sprawling tentacles has also been valuable, for chasing up any number of small details, ranging from London postcodes to cranio-facial duplication.

Lastly, I would like to thank John O'Brien of The Dalkey Archive Press and Andrew Russell of the Somerville Press: John, for his clear-thinking editorial commitment to *Huddleston Road* – he salvaged this short novel from the arms of a sprawling narrative mess while managing not to make me feel as though I was an idiot; and Andrew for introducing me and my work to the Dalkey Archive Press, and for generally looking after my interests.

JOHN TOOMEY, FEBRUARY 2012

Part I

Vic left Dublin for London when he was twenty-one. He'd been rattling about the place for a few years by then, going nowhere in particular. Having dropped out of two courses, a degree in journalism and a diploma in tourism, he'd found himself a three-day week in the local supermarket, working the fruit n' veg under the foulmouthed eye of a Belfast man, a good twenty years his senior.

Although the prospectless apprenticeship at the supermarket was never likely to last, it did, given his contribution-free tenancy with his parents, afford him a decent disposable income. So offdays were spent at the cinema, alone bar a handful of other lonely buffs, munching on popcorn and absorbing the gigantic intimacy of the virtually empty theatre. The aimlessness of it was apparent to him, but there was contentment too in those midweek hours nobody else had available to them.

In the evenings, during the week, when he wasn't out with friends who had determined to persist with third level education, he sat alone in his bedroom listening to albums over and over until he knew them inside out. He read biographies of famous musicians and actors, and struggled through the odd novel that he found reference to in somebody's life story. He wrote reams of self-indulgent poetry, and got drunk in the dark.

By the time of his twenty-first birthday he'd become restless, bored with himself. He ripped up and burned all the poetry and began to want for more, insisting to friends that what he craved were new encounters. He applied to several universities in England and, surprisingly, found that almost all of them were willing to accept him.

In mid-September, with his only fallback a phone number, he boarded a flight to London. The number was inscribed onto the inside cover of a hardback writing pad that he used for a journal. He drew a thick rectangle around it in red pen. The pad was about the only thing he deemed valuable among his travelling trinkets and clothes. Having by then forsaken poetry, he had begun to record, with meticulousness, the important and, it should be said, the mostly extraneous details of his life; substituting the purged poetry for pedestrian prose – one kind of conceitedness for another. He packed everything into a large rucksack and half expected to be back home by the New Year.

London and the university years were good to him. It thrilled and humbled, alternately. His journal entries from London were filled with a distinct excitement, constantly aquiver in every sentence. In those words, as self-obsessed and unexceptional as they read, the faintly recalled essence of scintillating promise was close to palpable; it was in the air each morning of that first winter, and in the warmth of the long May evenings where his gaze fell out the ramshackle sash-window, and across the park, with the sky ripening to red. Apprehension was bound up in there too, with all the emotions heightened by the experience of being out on his own, cut off from all homely comforts and security. London was everything he'd intended.

He stayed in halls of residence, sharing five storeys with a few hundred other students hailing from a range of cities and homelands. The only commonality they shared was the collective claim to have originated more than twenty-five miles from campus. The first few weeks were a blur of cheap beer, fleeting associations – feeling strangers out and up, wary of jumping in too quick with any one crowd – and looming loneliness.

Lectures, seminars and essays took a backseat, until the first round of assessments were handed back, stinging criticisms in tow, of the sort that propitious school teachers can never prepare you for. He came to realize his own ordinariness. Some people pack it in then – too much effort – and leave university with no degree and a student loan that was profligately squandered on booze, drugs and the rest. Others get their pride stung by near failure and pull the finger out. Vic surprised himself by falling in with the latter.

Despite his stated desire for new experiences, he survived largely within the confines of halls of residence and the route to campus, a closeted world of pseudo-reality; all that hippy idealism regarding the broadening of horizons was unrepentantly jettisoned in favour of subsidized student bars and frivolous associations. From time to time he took the Underground to Camden on a Sunday, or walked in. He ventured into Leicester Square and Oxford Street too, during that first winter, with a spirited group of fellow squatters from halls, to take in the seasonal lights. But there wasn't much more to his pursuit of the city's perspective.

Toward the end of the first semester, with the bitter cold outside and suffering some degree of malnutrition, he rang that number so carefully copied to the inside of his writing pad. His cousin Orla was the only person in the city he could consider family. She was ten or eleven years his senior and the last time he'd seen her was at her parents' twentieth wedding anniversary. He was five or six and she was a confident teenager, polite and assured. By the time he arrived in London she was married with two kids and living in Hampstead.

Although they could have passed on the street and not known each other, such was the time that had passed since they'd last met, Orla's innate geniality made quick work of any uncertainty. Within minutes she had invited him over for dinner. After nearly three months of toasted, cheap-cheese sandwiches, baked beans and beer, he enthusiastically accepted. Orla introduced him to her husband, Geoff, and the two kids. They were awfully bloody hospitable and charming. Had he not been so grateful, he might have been sickened by the greed – why must some people get it all? His super-animated recollection of Orla's blissful life could be dismissed as the famine induced hallucinations had it not been for the fact that the perfect looks, manners and fortune willfully withstood the weathering of the years; their perfection constantly adorning itself with still more resplendence and zest.

Their hospitality, in the thick of London's aloofness, affirmed Vic's faith in human kind. The ludicrously homely home in fashionable Hampstead became a safe-house for him; a place where his innards could be warmed by roast potatoes, vegetables and rare tastes of premium meat, so that he could return to student-world rejuvenated. In reciprocation, he babysat for them once a year, on their anniversary, when they would go out to dinner and see a show. A gesture of gratitude that over the course of his university years established itself as tradition.

With first year skippered successfully, and after spending a summer at home wondering whether he'd bother going back, he returned to London for his second year. He remained in halls of residence, as was his wont as an international student, and thus avoided all the pitfalls of renting in the open market with people you don't really know as well as you thought, and inevitably falling out with them in the kind of mini-dramas where the last dribble of semi-skimmed milk is a deal-breaker. There was more security for him in halls of residence. It afforded him a level of independence and solitude when needed, retreating to his room for days at a time when assignments needed writing, while also providing the opportunity to be with others at the bar, or share half an hour in the communal kitchen.

Knowing the ropes already, in a building populated mainly by first years, mostly kids fresh out of school, he was confident enough to resist rushing in. He stood back, mixed sparingly, and worked in a way that was more focused than before. By third year he was a seasoned student; an oasis of clarity and focus among the chaos and melodrama; a marvelous, sovereign entity in a vortex of sex and crying and puking. Occasionally, he cut loose and joined in, celebrating the end of each round of assignments.

The next step was just laziness. He'd enjoyed London and didn't want to leave. He didn't have the appetite for a Masters and he was, despite a degree, unqualified for everything. A few people he knew were going into teaching and he decided, in the absence of anything better, that it would do for him too. Accepted into another London university, he began the following September, his fourth in London, and trudged half-interestedly through a PGCE, passing with relative ease, and took up a post at Downwood the following September.

He met Lali at James' birthday celebration. At thirty, or soon to be, and with seven years service behind him, James was an old hand at Downwood. Vic, with only one full year in the job behind him, was still fairly fresh-faced and also, at twenty-five, still firmly in his youth. In a London school with an astonishingly high turnover of staff, James was considered an experienced teacher, and embraced the responsibility of such an impish title with appropriate rectitude; dismissing all his students as unthinking baboons, planning lessons on torn-off strips of cereal boxes, and meeting acronyms, initiatives or pilot anythings issued from the local council – ultimately dismissed as either 'unworkable' or 'fuckology' – with immeasurable contempt. James believed in the text, the power of a text itself. His first advice to Vic was, 'Pick a book you like, talk about why you like it. They'll learn more from that than a million storyboards, word searches, tableaux, role-plays or diary entries. And when you're done, pick something you hate. But make it short, an extract, and have a proper fucking rant about that. That's teaching.'

Vic came to notice her through a series of evanescent movements. She was something in his peripheral vision, a graceful flicker among the greater body of James' birthday guests. There was something about her coffee skin and jet black hair that beguiled. She was small and skinny, naturally skinny though, not in that anaemic, chronically delusional Hollywood starlet kind of way. 'She's an alright, girl. A bit feisty,' James said. Vic took this summation to be an endorsement, something James would later insist it was never intended as. Endorsement or disclaimer, it didn't matter. Vic would have taken his chances anyway. He swaggered across the flat, slinked his way onto the balcony, and stood between Lali and another man. 'Hi, I'm a friend of James'. From Downwood.'

Lali smiled and laughed a little. Promising, Vic thought. But then, devoid of modesty, she replied, 'Sorry, friend of James, but I don't do freckles.'

The bristling competition all but fell off the balcony laughing, and Lali stared contemptuously at him until he walked away. For weeks afterwards, Vic thought of all the things he should have said, all the lightning responses that might have redeemed him. But in the moment he was dumbstruck by the blatant arrogance of her assumptions.

For a while after the episode with Lali, he bore the scars of her malice. He was less sure of himself, and in worrying about how he stood or walked or spoke, he inadvertently contrived to make his every move ungainly and overtly self-conscious. In turn, this had the effect of making his conversation with girls in bars slump awkwardly to a standstill every time Lali's face revisited him, her clinical sneer sliced across it. They'd excuse themselves to the ladies, or anywhere, just to be free of Vic's unsettling babble, as he degenerated into chronic ineptitude.

He knew his confidence should be more robust and that Lali's reduction of him possessed no more sophistication than that of playground politics, but he struggled to dismiss it. And although in the rationality of his own mind he could overcome her and persevere, the memory of her affront retained the ability to undermine him at a glance.

The self-conscious inadequacy that Lali had unearthed in him was still dimly observable, several months later, when James set him up for dinner with another girl. James assured him that this was a 'good girl.' Vic nearly bolted at the sound of those words. But James convinced him that she was nothing like Lali.

They met in The Commons, in Blackheath, on a busy Friday, and she was sumptuous company. She was very interested in the fact that Vic was an English teacher, and wrongly assumed that he had extensive knowledge of his subject. She questioned him on novels and authors, and it became clear that the vivacious date was more widely read than the ambling English teacher. He bluffed his way through the literary minefield and then suggested they catch a train, or a taxi, into London and get something to eat.

The taxi set them down on Charing Cross Road. They agreed, since it was their first meal and there were no guarantees of anything, to go easy on Vic's wallet; the proviso being that were they to make it to a subsequent date, he'd have to push the boat out a little. So The Pizza Parlour it was.

A few hours later, Vic paid the bill and they walked out into London's winter evening. Students, groups of workers on nights out, theatre habitués, fell cheerfully in and out of restaurants and pubs.

The streetlights twinkled above them, the wind had calmed, and the rain, now only drizzling, trip-trapped on the ground. The promise of warm, musty-smelling pubs lured them through one last doorway.

When her phone rang, she looked at the screen apprehensively. 'I'm just going to take this outside. Home.' On her return she explained that she had to leave, candidly expounding, 'My father's sick. I said I'd be home by midnight.' It was just past one a.m.

She apologized and Vic asked for her number. She took his phone in her hand and tapped her name and number into his contacts. Pulling on her coat and buttoning up tight and warm, she leaned in and kissed him softly and wetly on the lips. He offered to take her home, but she declined.

He stayed a few minutes longer to finish his drink. As he stood up to leave he was met by a chesty stare; snarling, lithe, alluring. Lali was standing, her back against the bar, arms folded, cigarette between her fingers – cocked and wavering about her chin, as if poised to take another drag. A glass of wine in her other hand was tucked in beneath her elbow. He sighed and, in uncertainty, looked behind him to make sure she wasn't looking at somebody else. But there was nobody. The bar was emptying as people began to choose between clubs and night-buses.

With a fleetness of foot that only men so flippantly spurned can know, he turned to take his coat from the stool. But as he turned back around Lali was standing beside him, a pint in one hand, which she placed down beside his empty glass, and her own drink and cigarette in her other. She sat down on the vacated stool, kicked her right leg over her left knee, and said, 'Sit down. Have a drink. On me.' He looked at her in unimpressed disbelief. Somebody from the crowd of people she had been with was mouthing something at her. 'Relax,' she shouted over. 'I'll buy you another.' He was still standing, still not quite gone. 'Oh, sit down. Come on,' she said. 'Did I scare you that much?'

'No thanks,' he replied. He started to go, fixing his coat.

She stood up quickly and took hold of his arm and turned him towards her. She seemed taller than he remembered. 'Come on, James' friend, have a drink with me. One drink.' There was something kinder in her voice and it was unexpected. She asked for his name – the bare-faced cheek.

With the drinks knocked back and the bar closing, he accepted her invitation back to a party in her flat. The party raged on into the small hours. It was five, or later, before Lali directed him to her bedroom, pushing and shifting him by the hips, from behind, through the made up beds, and the empty cans and bottles, and the leaden bodies of the collapsed, that were strewn across the floor.

The bedroom was lit by a tiny lamp in the corner of her room. With the door closed behind them, she backed him to the edge of the bed, and gently but forcefully tipped him over. She hovered over him. Precariously. Pouting suggestively. She nuzzled her knee between his legs as he lay on the bed looking up at her. She leaned down, still looking into his eyes, and unbuckled his belt and undid the first two buttons of his jeans. Her black hair fell down over his hips. Then she stood up, as if drunkenly forgetting her routine, and began unbuttoning her top. She tossed it to the corner of the room and stood there above him in her bra, his partially unbuttoned trousers left like a job half done. Then she undid her own, let them slide down her thighs and drop onto her ankles, bunching up around her soaring heels, before stepping out of them and kicking them to one side. She stood for a moment, in her underwear and shoes, swaying drunkenly above him in the amber lamplight. It was something other-worldly – the abandon of those hours preserved in that image of her, that iconic pose. He was in a haze. Her body, burnt umber against her brilliant white underwear, and the anticipation, imprinted itself on his psyche, and remained there through all the years and discolouring experiences that followed. She lowered herself again, undid the last buttons, and slid his trousers and underwear off in one go. Her long hair rained down black on his midriff, once again, crashing from a height onto his alabaster thighs, lucently pale next to her cheek, and cascading over his hips, as he undid his shirt, wriggled free of it, and flung it at the foot of the bed.

A firm and repetitive slapping of his cheek brought him round.

'Time to get up.'

'Seriously?'

'Yeah. I'm already late.'

Awake then, Vic surprised himself with his capacity for small talk. He felt altered, physically, by having slept with her. He was conscious of how his breath now filled the depth of his lungs. Conscious of standing taller, and of speaking less dementedly. It was as if he had stolen back what she had taken from him.

She was on her way to work, she said, and advised him that it would be better if he left the flat before her flatmate got up. She didn't explain any further and was oblivious to Vic's renewed self-possession. She herded him from the bedroom with a steady flow of prompts: 'Here's your trousers . . . Here's your shirt . . . Shoe's over there . . . Are we good to go? . . . Station's at the top of the road . . .'

There was further urgency in her manner as she picked up his coat from the arm of the sofa and handed it to him, brushing her hair as they walked to the door. He tried a little more small talk but she didn't have the time. He leaned in and kissed her and she let their lips meet, flatly, and then withdrew, before offering the kind of smile you might get from an elderly aunt; disingenuous, intangibly dismissive. The illusion of self-possession that he'd enjoyed only moments before, corrected itself.

Within ten minutes he was standing alone at Deptford Station, feeling strangely stunned. It was cold and he was sleep-deprived, and still a little drunk. The first stage of the journey, on an empty train to London Bridge, was undignified enough, but the twenty minute bus journey to Camberwell was torturous. It seemed to creep from stop to stop and take five minutes at each one, offloading and boarding no more than a handful of passengers. Riding on the shuddering swagger of the bus's vibration, he slipped between peaceful half-dreams and lewd remembrances.

Then he missed his stop. He woke up at Denmark Hill and cursed every yard back to Camberwell Green. Once home, he fell asleep with the Saturday sports on his chest and a half-eaten bacon sandwich by the side of the bed. He slept well into the afternoon. Sometime in early evening, completely disorientated by the fractured day, he came back to life. Awake and thinking more lucidly, he began to consider Lali, to remember events and apply meaning.

When James phoned, Vic divulged everything. Boastfully.

'I'm glad you've got the gloating out of your system. Now, what about this evening?' James asked.

'I think I'll stay in.'

'Bad idea. Terrible fucking idea, mate.'

'Why? Watch Match of the Day, have a beer, maybe. Enjoy my Sunday.'

'Oh no, Vic. This is all wrong.'

'I got all my work done last night. What more could I realistically gain from the weekend?'

'A clear mind, that's what. You stay in and you're fucked. At best you'll have a miserable week ahead, wishing and wondering.'

'I don't see that. I'd just like to have a quiet night.'

'No, no, no. If you stay in you're going to end up replaying last night in your head. It's all going to start looking fantastic as you sit in alone with nothing but football and shit beer. You've lost all perspective, mate. You need to come out and get rejected by a handful of girls and go home with a fat one. You need to demystify last night. She skewed everything by waking you before you'd even had the chance to have a hangover.'

'I'm staying in.'

'Never let the memory of last night's tramp prevent you from nailing tonight's. You know who said that?'

'Robert Frost?'

'No. A man with no worries, Vic. A man who knows the limits of men. Me. I said it.'

'Goodnight, James.'

James had read the situation accurately enough, although his prediction that Vic would be near collapse by midweek was overblown. Lali did occupy his thoughts, and more so as the week progressed. He tried, at length, to recall her face. In obsessive detail – from the isotropic flawlessness of her nose and cheeks to the dark iris of her eyes, to the pores of her peachy chin and the hairline nick of scar tissue on the curve of her jaw.

Even travelling to work, on public transport, when the form, smell and sound of an attractive woman would appear in his field of vision, he could objectively appreciate her attractiveness, only for Lali to intrude. The objective beauty of a stranger on a train became suddenly wooden when placed in the context of Lali's animated exaltation. Her beauty transcended any kind of dispassion and had already begun to inhabit a space in his soul that was both real and aspirational.

His conversations with James in the week that followed were like archaeological digs, careful and slow, without any obvious yield. He learned that she owned and managed the coffee shop where she worked. 'For a good few years, at least,' James said. 'In Greenwich, but she's a North London girl. I knew her little in the early days.'

When James spoke of the early days what he was recalling were his years as a stray in London. He'd travelled from Swansea with nothing but a paperback novel stuffed into his jacket and worked in various areas of the service industry to get by.

'She was sleeping with a friend of mine, on and off,' he told Vic. On the subject of Lali's flatmate, who Vic never met and wrongly imagined to be a male friend, James told him he had no idea who she lived with or what her eagerness to have Vic out of the flat might have been about. 'Who knows, Vic? I'm telling you, leave this notch on the bedpost. The fuck of your life. Now move on.'

'Why do you need to punctuate every sentence with filth?'

'I punctuate my sentences with facts, my Celtic cousin. Look, you fucked her, she fucked you. Who cares? The point is that you need now to forget about her. Anything else is just your ego. She hasn't asked for anything more, and she has atoned for her very public humiliation of you. Leave it there, I say.' James stood up from a stack of loose pages on the desk before him as he said this, drawing the conversation to a close. 'Have I ever told you that I hate teaching? I've run out of red pen for all the inadequacies of this lot. A set of papers two inches high, with answers twice as fucking thick!'

By the middle of the week, he was refusing to engage with Vic at all. Vic had probed, directly and indirectly, and relentlessly, in pursuit of some missing essence of Lali, to the point that James lost patience. He was no longer able to conceal his irritation with Vic's interest in Lali and declared, 'I'm done now, Vic. Okay? I'm not talking to you, about anything, until she's off the table.'

Vic's solution to this impasse was to spend a Saturday morning on a self-directed walking tour of Greenwich. It wasn't long before he spotted Lali through the glass facade of a trendily poky coffee shop. She was behind a counter, taking money at the till.

He bought a paper from the kiosk on the far side of the street and sat down on the wall. Pretending to read the sports, he watched her as she worked, shuttling between till and tables, and then behind the counter where she was hardly visible for the shine on the window. The name above the shop was in a royal blue, baroque scrawl – Rococo's. He wondered did she inherit the name with the premises and was unsure whether it mattered.

Every time he caught a glimpse of her, he remembered and had to look away, unnerved by the voyeuristic composition of his burgeoning obsession. He got lost for minutes at a time, pretending to read his newspaper.

Just as he began to think it would be a better idea to forget about her, beginning to doubt the veracity of his recollections – time had surely embellished the experience – a pair of plump feet appeared on the path in front of him. Looming over him was a large woman in her late twenties, or early thirties, maybe, with curly brown hair. She handed him a cardboard cup with tea in it.

'On the house, she says.'

'Thanks.'

'She said she owes you a breakfast.'

The large girl turned, looked right and left, and crossed the street and went back into Rococo's. When he entered the shop, Lali was busy with a couple of customers at the till. He took a sip of the tea and tried to control the palpitations, the racing adrenaline of embarrassment and trepidation. Then he presented himself to her, wide open and breath held.

'Take a seat,' she said. 'I'll take my break.'

Vic took a seat at an empty four-seater table by the window and heard her call into the kitchen, 'Continental breakfast, tea, large coffee, and a muffin, Aldo. Table two.'

She untied and removed her apron and sat across from him.

Her eyes looked tired but intense; inquisitive, street-smart, hazel whirls of impenetrable murk. The shop was warm and the straps of her black bra were visible on her shoulders from beneath her casual, grey vest-top. Her bare arms revealed skin as sleek and toned as he remembered. Swept back off her forehead by a hair-band, her lustrous mane, fixed in a hurry, was slightly less perfect than the rest of her.

She lit a cigarette but said nothing. Vic looked back at her, posing as if calm and cool but actually clammed-up and unable to speak. Having come so far in pursuit of her and having then found himself paralysed, he was on the verge of standing up and walking out, without explanation, afraid that the frenzied flicker in his eyes had already betrayed him.

But then she broke the silence with the kind of simple salutation that he had been pathetically incapable of. 'So, how've you been, Vic?'

He received those simple words with disproportionate gratitude and they continued from there, for several vapid minutes, exchanging equally mundane conversation starters that somehow failed to have the desired effect. Eventually it was James, their only common point of intersection, that succeeded in moving the conversation from this rut.

'Let's not dwell on things,' she said, putting her hand on his at the mention of James' party. The gesture halted any recriminations. It appeased, softened her in his eyes, and also seemed to transform the previously inconsequential encounter to one of intimate significance; it felt like there was some kind of history at work, the way her hand touched his and asked him to look forward now, to forget what couldn't be helped.

They were soon interrupted by Aldo, a short and scrawny and heavily bestubbled man about Vic's age, delivering the breakfasts. Lali took her coffee and lit up another cigarette, looking across at Vic as he ate. With her cocky indifference, she bound him in another silence. Vic was just noting the imbalanced dynamic at work between them, wondering whether it could be considered a pattern at this early stage, when she let him off the hook again.

'There's a party next week. A friend of mine. Why don't you come along?'

The invitation redeemed her, redeemed them both. It allowed them to talk some more, for him to ask questions, to have something to say. The tremors and licks of her beautiful face in motion was given body and realness by her taut voice.

Then, at a point, it occurred to Vic that he would like to leave, that the breakfast with Lali was a decent start and it was time to withdraw and regroup. He sensed that another uncomfortable silence was on its way, when the plump girl from earlier arrived tableside, telling Lali there was a call.

Lali stubbed out her cigarette and introduced Vic to Donna. 'I'll call you during the week,' Lali said to him, as she stood up.

It was just Vic and Donna then; her, a wall of reticence. Before he had a chance to take his leave, Donna lifted his unfinished breakfast from the table and left.

The following Saturday came but with no haste. The week was pock-marked by Lali's intrusion into almost every waking thought. Vic considered what it was about her, specifically. His attraction to her was underpinned by what seemed to him a purely salacious motivation. At the same time, his need for her was not the simple stuff of anonymous lust, taking her and leaving her. He wanted more of her than just that, but a long habit of conformity required him to search for some other, deeper motivation. It didn't necessarily need to be love, he told himself, just something more profound than carnality.

Lali, though, appeared completely at ease with the shallowness of it. She almost reveled in the debased individualism. The inherent self-indulgence of such promiscuity hung from her delicate shoulders like a chiffon dress, and, somehow, her disregard for etiquette enhanced her irresistibility. It liberated her to do things like just sit and watch him eat, and take unusual pleasure in the rising panic of his eyes. She could do that because what was useful in him wasn't sacred; it could be found throbbing somewhere in the minds and between the legs of *any* man. If Vic didn't fuck her, somebody else would.

Vic spent much time trying to make a better story than that of her. Something that would ameliorate the arrogance, make sense of her ardent dislocation. But his efforts were wholly unsuccessful and he reached the Saturday of the party more perplexed by her incompleteness than he had been at the beginning of the week. Somehow, peering into the depths of Lali made her less comprehensible.

Vic eventually convinced James that the party's opportunities outweighed the folly of Vic's ambition, and he agreed to go along. They met at London Bridge before taking the Underground to Archway. The journey gifted James a captive audience and he took the opportunity to impress upon Vic his gloomy prognosis; without a single specific detail or incidence of proof, he forcefully implied Lali's unsuitability. He discouraged Vic, repeatedly, without ever actually defaming her.

'I just don't see it, mate,' James reasoned.

'See what? We're just meeting up to see how it goes.'

'I don't like the balance of this dalliance,' he said. 'You started on the back-foot and now . . . ' He had to pull his head back in as another passenger passed toward the door with the Underground rattling and heaving to a stop. When she had passed and he had looked her up and down, he leaned back across, elbows on his knees and his head jutting across the carriage at Vic. The doors hissed and closed, and the dry grime of the Underground was in the air, as James picked up his point. 'I just don't think a girl like this is for you.'

Vic raised an eyebrow, quizzical, and sceptical.

'From what I know, I don't like it,' James continued, then paused. 'I can't have my wingman in a relationship. She's already fucked up one Saturday night.'

'Let's just go to the party,' Vic responded.

'I'm not holding your hand here, mate. If you go around moping . . . I'm here for women. Pure and simple. Friendship is for weekdays.'

It was a typical North London house; tall, narrow, three floors and an attic. It seemed to be falling apart from the inside; cobwebs in high corners, cracked plaster on the ceilings, a wafer blanket of dust on every surface, manky furnishings, drafty windows and crocked doors. But above all the mess, in every room, the walls were dressed in the wildest paintings; violently vibrant in colour, curlicues and hard edges thrown together, parts of images merging with seas of indiscriminate pattern and chaos. They were arresting and incomprehensible, and juxtaposed against their creator, and the evening's host, who was typical. You would have guessed what he looked like just by the aspirations of his work; tall, gaunt, elaborately limbed, flowing scarf, dismissive of the minions on one hand and fawning on the other.

Lali was sitting on the artist's lap when they arrived. She had a glass of wine in her hand, dancing in the air to the rhythm of her seduction – in to her lips for a suggestive sip and then waltzing back out to the beat of her vexing refrain. The artist looked enthralled, his own party playing out around him, without him, as she wrapped his overlong scarf one more time around his neck.

When Vic caught her eye, she curled her lip and nodded at him. He acknowledged her with a casual wave but when she just turned back to the artist, Vic was left wondering what to do with his hand, now that it was out there, conspicuously. He glanced about for James, but he was already moving away toward a group of mostly girls by the fireplace.

As he watched Lali kiss the artist, Vic was already on his way to the door. But then she stood up, patted the artist with condescending lightness upon the cheek, pulled her skirt straight, and walked over to Vic. She gently moved people to the side as she crossed the room; parting human seas to ruin him.

There were no awkward kisses on the cheek. She kissed Vic on the lips, just like she had kissed artist, only these lips were Vic's, and asked, 'Alright?'

She came and went over the course of hours and Vic didn't feel as lost as he usually would in a house of strangers. James disappeared around midnight, out the door with two giggling girls and some old Uni friend he'd met. He pleaded with Vic to come with him and sighed when Vic opted, instead, to remain talking with a group of strangers, waiting for Lali to come back to him, to sustain him for another hour.

Some time later she descended on him, drunk and amorous, and ushered him to a bedroom. She closed the door behind them and led him to the bed. She leaned intently against him until he toppled onto it. He was among a pile of coats. She reached through the darkness and placed a hand on his chest, then crawled on top of him. As she straddled him, Vic could feel her sharp heels digging into his thighs. He felt her breath in his ear and the flesh of her cleavage resting on his chin. She whispered, 'We need to find my coat. It's home time.'

It seemed familiar, already.

One Saturday night became two, and three, and gradually developed into whole weekends spent together. As the weekends then crept into the weekdays, Vic came to stay over at her flat a couple of evenings during the week. Their social circles started to contract and amalgamate, and they became something more than casual.

Vic felt as though he was acquiring what he had sought from the start, an understanding of who she was, of her mystery. The mere accumulation of time spent together gave him a false sense of knowing. He thought that in meeting more of her friends and browsing her music collection, and knowing how she took her coffee and what she wore to bed, that he was getting closer to her.

He mistook, in a very modern way, information for knowledge.

He thought that having visited Buckingham Palace together, for instance, and worked out that they both liked the horses, that he liked some of the paintings and she just didn't care, and that neither of them had any interest in the gardens, that they were in some way known to each other. And this feeling was buttressed by its location in one of her energetic, gregarious phases. A time when Vic had forgotten the flippant meanness that she had first shown to him.

She was busy and dynamic, engrossed in the project that was the prying open of his closeted world, his self-contained and tiny contentment. Vic imagined that he must have seemed quaint to her, a young man of roughly her age but utterly anachronistic; he didn't embrace London's vastness, preferring, instead, to survive in tiny pockets of the place that were familiar and safe. He didn't like clubs or any kind of music that didn't involve a guitar, and he certainly didn't like city tours. He was swallowed up by the city, in many respects, softly anonymous among the flash and the tittup. Not lonely exactly, or independent, but not unhappy either.

The visit to the Palace was one of her attempts to broaden Vic's world.

'I thought you were a man of *education*,' she said, as if that was the trammel to catch him.

'I've no interest.'

'You don't have to curtsy to Her Majesty on the way through or anything,' she gibed.

As they walked along Constitutional Hill, flanked on the right by Buckingham Palace Gardens and on the left by Green Park, Vic began honing in on the core of his disgruntlement. 'It's the false reverence of the term. That bowed-head kind of paying homage . . . I mean what has she ever done? You pay for all her privilege with your taxes. With my bloody taxes! And just because somebody decided that they were a special family hundreds of years ago, or because they killed off some other family that thought they were special. I don't get it. It infuriates me. The French had the right idea – lynch the bastards!' he finished, bringing his loosely conceived republican tirade to an end as they came to the gates of the palace.

'That's beautiful, Vic,' she said, a little impatiently. 'Now, come on.'

The frisky argumentativeness, characteristic of what they seemed to be developing into, emboldened Vic's trust in Lali. His initial fear that their relationship lacked commonality was allayed by the feeling that their differences might turn out to be as capable of sustaining them as any illusive commonality. This promise stripped her unpredictability of its foreboding, freed him to invest everything in her honed aesthetic.

The extravagance and decadence of the palace confirmed for him the righteousness of his indignation. 'A gold effing coach!' he hissed into her ear, as they toured the Royal Mews. The royal collection held not a single painting he recognized but he enjoyed the hour of culture he would otherwise have ignored. The horses, pronounced in their muscularity and bay colouring, were less contentiously impressive; naturally awesome, dignified, and calm as they trotted past. But beyond the horses and the art, there was only what they dismissed as the royal shrubbery and pigeons, and Lali wasn't for pretence. Her anarchical impatience had them through the gardens and on their way down Buckingham Palace Road, towards Victoria Station, before Vic could voice his own disinterest. They stopped for cigarettes and Lali grinned at him as she lit up. 'You see, I could be good for you.'

To Vic, this was further encouragement. It indicated that she had a future, for starters, and that she considered *him* a part of it. It suggested that he wasn't out there alone, laid bare; she was too. For the first time, his conception of her existing in a state of perpetual certainty fell away, and she stood before him like anyone else – self-doubting, reliant on nothing more substantial than hope, or a gut feeling for the decency of the person you chose to be with. It was as if she wanted to let Vic in, as if there was an *in*.

On the Underground home there was only standing room and the noise of the rickety carriages meant they didn't try to speak. Lali just hung her arms around his waist and plunged her hands into the back pockets of his jeans, as he held them steady on an overhead rail. Another gesture. Meaningless, perhaps, but not lost on him. She leaned against him for a few minutes; almost but not quite a perfect metaphor for love. It was enough to convince him of what he wanted to believe. Then, on the train to Deptford, they managed to get seats and they both closed their eyes.

During the first months Lali was more or less the girl she seemed from the outset – fleetingly mean with a turn of phrase, but confident, unpredictable and breathtaking. They attended informal dinner parties, visited all the naff tourist attractions that Vic had never bothered with, picnicked in Hyde Park on roasting summer days, went pubbing and clubbing, went to concerts, and took long weekends away in Cornwall and Southampton.

Lali revealed herself by degrees. Information, a story, a memory would emerge from her, and he was allowed a few quick questions before she shut the lid on it again. The purposefully obscured depths of her, and the false impression of intimacy, were illuminated by her discretional revelations.

Lali's uncloaking of her grandmother was the most notable of the early disclosures. Vic was shocked, first by the discovery that Lali had a family, and only then by the fact that it had taken him that long to notice she'd never spoken of them. What was it about her that precluded those questions? he later wondered. How was it that she could stand before him in all her beauty without ever prompting him to ask, Where have you come from? What forces of human fusion created you?

'Gail used to do this to me,' she told him, raking her fingers through a matted clump of his hair as they lay in bed. His head was tilted back and lay on her breast bone. Her fine, toothy fingers glided through his hair, as if she were mapping the potted and lumped landscape of his skull. She smoothed it back, first into a quiff and then flattening it further with each stroke; long, weaving movements across his cranium. 'To relax me.'

'And who's Gail?'

'My grandmother.'

Having quickly established that Gail was not long dead, as was natural for him to have assumed, given the months they had been together and this was Lali's first mention of her, he sat up in the bed. 'I can't believe I never asked any of this,' he said, aloud and to himself. 'Are there others?'

'No. Just Gail.' There was nothing in Lali's voice, not pain or resolve, just an impervious matter of fact. 'I'm up early in the morning, by the way. Stock-take.'

She rolled away from him and turned on the bedside lamp, rupturing the moment. In the dull glow her remarkable symmetry was enhanced, but the moment had been quashed. The conversation was over. She took some nail varnish from the bedside locker and began painting her toes.

Then there were the stories that recurred. He heard many times about how, as a child, she had escaped Gail's watchful eye and hid among the bushes and trees that lined the path through the park. She watched the people as they passed and read a million stories into their facial expressions, gestures and mannerisms; a formidable capacity to unearth the lugubrious in the mundane, finding its beginning. He didn't know how old she would have been but he could imagine her, observing and questioning. Couples, small families, old people, even children – 'They all made me feel hopeless,' she told him. Though what she meant was sad, or melancholy. It wasn't what they did or how they acted, she said. 'It was their state of . . . What awaits whoever. The inevitability.'

'Being human,' he sometimes put to her. 'To wonder what it's all for.'

'I hate it. I fucking hate it,' she repeated, as if his interjection had gone unheard. And then she was back – strong, defensive, unforgiving. As before. Without sympathy, even for herself.

The first seismic shift in her came unannounced. They had been in Marlowe's, in Catford, the night before. A karaoke night experiment.

Vic saw the DJ warming up – peach shirt tucked into his jeans, beer gut, hair slicked back, running through a few lines of his favourite crooner classics – and he thought, Oh no, this isn't going to work out.

There was Lali and Donna, and a few of their staff from Rococo's, and Vic had asked James and a couple of other friends from Downwood to come along.

Donna was her usual abrupt self, which Vic put down to it being her weekend to open up Rococo's for Saturday business, and so tainting her Friday night with the prospect of an early morning. But Lali was at her most vivacious.

Crammed into a corner of the packed pub, they were all sitting on top of each other. Lali was buying drinks for everyone, kissing Vic across the table, or squeezing his arse as she passed behind him to the ladies, while he stood talking football at the bar with some burly, tattooed stranger. He indulged the moment. There was still so much to be enjoyed, so much newness and excitement to them. That night in Marlowe's he just wanted to enjoy Lali as she was – infectiously energetic, sultry, drunk.

But he refused to sing. He was adamant. He couldn't.

'You've got to do this,' she insisted. They were at the bar, away from the others, and she was leaning all her weight against him. She puckered up, pleading mock-submissively. 'Please, Vic? It'll be fun. Don't be an asshole!'

'Seriously, I can't sing,' he told her, again.

'Don't be a fucking grouch, Vic! It's karaoke – nobody can sing. Come on, we'll find you a good old Irish rebel song. No need to sing them, you just growl 'em,' she said.

'In all seriousness, now, you don't want me to sing,' he warned her.

'I'll make it worth your while,' she said, tugging his lower lip with her teeth as she broke away.

'Elaborate.'

'Vic, there's a lot more to come, believe me.'

When they went back to the table Lali put her drink down and strutted up to the raised platform. She said a few words and the karaoke man handed her the mike. It crackled as she switched it on. 'This one's for my man, Vic.' Fiddle and drum came barreling out of the speakers, and Lali, bow-legged and elbows out, rocking on the pins of her majestic heels in simulation of the choppy sea, did her finest sea-beaten sailor impression, while growling out lyrics in the worst Irish accent he'd ever heard – *The Irish Rover*. When she'd finished, she took a bow to lively applause from their table.

She held Vic's regard as she crossed the floor, until her attention was caught by two men. One of two brave suitors had said something to her over his shoulder. It caused her to stop and turn back.

Without the grip of Lali's gaze, an undistorted vision actualized. Existing momentarily outside himself, he saw what the cold-eyed observer would see; all eyes had followed Lali from the stage across the floor, and all eyes now watched, apprehensively, to see what happened to the brave. The power of her, the draw, was demonstrable. It was evident in the nervousness she set off in other people. Her stupefying beauty, as every eye in the room looked on, cried out across the room, commoving and stifling simultaneously.

They circled her then; somehow, with just the two of them they circled her. They were drawn in close about her as she spoke. He couldn't see her face but he could imagine it as he watched the two men gaping back at her and jostling for her attention; clinking glasses, throwing fraternal arms around each other, trying to reach out to her with searching touches. Whatever she finally said to them, it caused feigned offence. They raised their palms to her and leaned back with contorted expressions, and everyone breathed easy. As she ambled back to the table, unaware of the ripples of relief flowing, like a wedding train, back through the room behind her, Vic felt exhilarated by his closeness to her. Once back at the table, she promptly sent out the call for a round of shots.

They stumbled into her flat around three in the morning, made toasted cheese sandwiches and did what all couples at that stage of knowing each other do.

When Vic awoke in the morning, his throat was raspy. He leaned over her and whispered in her ear. Obviously suffering, she remained entombed under the duvet. He left the flat for the local mini-market.

He hoped that by the time he got back she'd have come round and they'd pick up where they left off the night before. But when he returned, the latch was on the door. He rang the bell. He called in the letterbox. It was all he could do just to get her out of bed and let him back into the flat.

Finally, she staggered to the door with the duvet wrapped around her, pulled up over her head so that only a few unkempt strands of tangled hair could be seen, as they drooped down over one of her eyes and across her nose. She turned the key, undid the latch, and let him in.

'Oh,' she sighed, 'you're back.'

'That's nice,' he replied.

She turned and went for the sofa, where she lay out. 'I thought you were gone,' she said, turning on the TV.

'I told you where I was going. To get us breakfast. I got some bacon and eggs. I'll make breakfast.'

'Go ahead.'

'I meant for the both of us. I'll make breakfast for the both of us.'

'Not for me.'

The offhandedness unsettled him but he made her coffee anyway.

'I told you – I don't want anything!' was her irascible response.

He placed it down on a coaster on the floor beside the sofa. In the kitchenette, he fried breakfast for himself and took it to the living area on a plate. After hovering around the sofa, thinking she might lift her feet and make room for him, and being disappointed, he took a seat in the only other proper chair in the flat. It was a battered old chair in the corner of the room, with no view of the TV.

'Is there anything on?' He waited. 'No?'

'Oh,' she said, surprised he was talking to her. 'No. Nothing.'

'Jesus, I'm fairly wrecked today. Heavy old night, last night.'

'Hmm?'

'Heavy night, I said. A lazy day ahead I'd imagine. I wouldn't be fit for much else.'

She said nothing.

With his appetite lost, he gave up and took the breakfast to the kitchen and dumped the plate, unrinsed and including the food, into the sink. He told her he was going home for a shower and a change of clothes.

'Oh, right.'

'Have you any plans for later? For tonight?' he asked, with saintly reserve, making one last attempt to wrest some sense from the confounding experience that was the night before and the morning after; a single happening, yet completely discrepant.

'No.'

She was impregnable in her quilted cocoon.

He went home wondering what he'd done wrong. She'd just flipped. They had dropped off to sleep, spooned air-tightly together, with his hand lightly caressing her upper-thigh. No worse than light snoring had passed between them, but when he awoke she'd transmogrified; alien, dislocated.

For a moment he did what all men do when they've just slept with a woman who fails to express sufficient gratitude – he wondered had he been no good. Did she lie there awake after he'd fallen asleep, wanting more? Disappointed? Unsatisfied? Or had her head been turned by the two men at Marlowe's? Had she grown tired of him already?

Several days passed before she called him. She was at Rococo's when she rang, which provided her with a conveniently short window for conversation. She asked whether he'd like to come over for dinner with her and Donna; some Thai food and a film.

When he asked was she okay, attempting to open up the issue of her irrational indifference to him, she evaded it. She had customers to attend to, she said, and needed to go. 'But come over,' she insisted.

Her insistence on him coming over put his mind at rest. She'd been out of order and she just wanted to move on, he thought. It was as good as an apology.

* * *

An invitation to Geoff's forty-fifth birthday was met with suspicion and reluctance. It had been extended as a matter of courtesy, after Vic had told Orla about Lali. Vic viewed it as an opportune occasion for Lali's casual induction; a few drinks and some finger food.

'I don't think so,' was Lali's response.

She moved then from not wanting to go, to the barely more substantial inability to go. She cited a pre-existing arrangement with Donna for the same night.

Vic saw the excuse for what it was and called it as such: a sham. He tried to impress on Lali the significance of Orla, and the decency of her. But Lali could be moved to nothing through obligation.

Then the girls, Lali and Donna, fell out in a dispute over working hours. Lali cut Donna to pieces, turning on her closest friend for having the gall to question the roster. It was so personal that Vic suspected their friendship was over. Donna objected to being rostered for both the Saturday and the Sunday, and was unusually adamant that it was Lali's turn to open up on the Saturday.

'Owner's prerogative, surely,' Vic said.

'Exactly! She said I was taking advantage. I've been carrying that whale since we were kids. And I pay her well. Especially considering she's a fucking liability.'

'Is that the line of diplomacy you went with?'

'Not exactly.' Then, beginning to laugh, Lali said, 'But I did threaten to take her doughnut allowance away.'

Donna irritated Vic greatly. She seemed always to be in the

way. To a significant degree, and wrongly, he viewed her as an obstruction. So he laughed along, indulging Lali's cruelty, because it suited. And because it was always nice to know, with certainty, that you were on the same side as Lali.

'But now you have to open up yourself, Saturday and Sunday,' he said, thinking that any chance of her accompanying him to Orla's was gone for sure. But Lali always had a distinctive logic, distinctive in its utter deficit of reason.

'Yeah, but I suppose that means I can come to your cousin's lame party now.'

He just accepted. 'Good. We're to be there for eight.'

He met her after work and as they made their way back to her flat she was quiet. He had been braced for resistance, or manic hyperactivity, fuelled by earlier than usual drinks, but not for her open but seemingly unconscious lassitude.

At her flat, Vic began by showering and dressing, and having something small to eat, while Lali pulled her knees into her chest and propped her head on some cushions on the sofa. The sound of the TV lapped over her and there was no indication that she would initiate anything any time soon. He wondered was she pre-occupied by her fight with Donna, or whether she was daunted by the prospect of meeting his cousin and her family, by a perceived formality of occasion. Whatever it was, a morose stillness hung about her. Then, around a quarter to eight, she finally began readying herself. Vic said nothing, resisting the urge to move her along more swiftly.

On the doorstep of Orla's house, with the doorbell already rung, Lali spoke. 'So what do these people do with themselves?'

Through the frosted glass of the front door Vic could see the undefined shape of Orla coming down the hall. Rushed and ill-prepared, he condensed what he knew down to as few words as possible. 'Orla writes. And she's a mum. Geoff's some kind of I.T. genius. They're nice,' he assured her. 'You'll be fine.'

Although Lali had turned to face the door as Orla opened it, she didn't have time or wasn't inclined to replace the look on her face with anything better. Orla's welcome stuttered, confronted by Lali's indiscriminate glare. But Orla promptly regained her composure and welcomed them both, ushering them into the hallway.

Lali managed a muted hello and handed Orla the bottle of wine. Taking their coats, Orla called into the living room for Geoff. His mop of gritty blond hair, beginning to whiten and grey, framed his cheerful face, as he reached out for a manly handshake and clapped Vic on the shoulder. 'Now, how did you fool this beautiful lady into accompanying you?'

Geoff's mild flirtation soothed Lali's tension, but she remained on Vic's shoulder for most of the evening. She sipped away quietly on glasses of wine as Vic tried to integrate himself among the guests. On several occasions, Vic discovered Orla beside him, offering crudités, tiny quiche slices, canapés, filled tortilla wraps, or more wine, and softly enquiring how they were doing. She seemed aware of Lali's discomfort. Vic encouraged Orla to go and enjoy the party herself. Lali's sole acknowledgement of Orla's concern was to shift her gaze from whatever absent task it had set itself. Once she smiled, but in a manner that seemed insincere.

Nervousness. Fear, maybe, came next. An anxiety regarding the unknown came over him – what would she do now? how should he react or intercept? He felt Lali drift off his shoulder, word by word. He could feel the menace of her head beginning to lift, the bravery of inebriation. Before he knew it she was wading into the small crowd of visitors, becoming more loquacious with each step.

Vic was talking with Geoff, watching her carefully, when she stumbled against a bookcase, trying to squeeze toward the hall-way. She bounced off it and put her hand out to steady herself. It worked but as she took hold of some woman's arm it sent the woman's drink down the front of her top and caused her to screech. Lali's apology echoed hollowly below her hysterical laughter. The woman did her best to remain calm. But when Lali saw the look of annoyance on her face, she had what she desired – indignation!

'What's your fucking problem?' she snarled. 'I apologized. It was an accident.'

'My top is ruined,' the woman began, expecting, surely, to be the aggrieved in this situation, but finding that the Lali was already sky-high on a victim complex.

Lali leered toward her. 'It's just a bit of wine.'

Vic moved across the room, apace, to lead Lali away before it descended into worse. She shuffled along, with minimal resis-tance, but kept looking to Vic and then away, toward the woman's tie-dye wine stain, and back again, in disgust.

While Lali puffed and sulked in the hall, not sure where to be-gin her assault but certain that she would, Vic waved Orla away to fetch their coats.

'Be easier if we left, would it?' Lali challenged, as Orla returned with the coats over her arm.

'I'm not sending you away,' Orla said, defensively. 'I thought you might want to.'

'Why? Because you want me to?'

'I asked her to get our coats, Lali. You've made an arse of yourself,' Vic cut in.

'I've made an *arse* of myself?' she said, stressing the idiom, as if the expression was the essence of a xenophobic ganging-up; the very language they used excluding her, making her feel inept. 'I'm the asshole?' Then she turned her attention back toward Orla. 'It was an accident. They happen. Probably not at parties like these, but they happen all the time. And I apologized, for fuck sake!'

'Calm down,' Orla said.

'Calm down? Why don't you calm down, you spoiled bitch!' Lali snatched her coat and turned for the door.

Vic called out and walked a few steps in pursuit of her, but she was moving too fast. 'Lali,' he shouted after her as she walked out. 'What do you want me to do here?' She wasn't hearing anyone.

Orla, standing behind him, let an involuntary sigh. Confounded, they both watched as Lali faded away among the dim street lights, passed over the road and flitted in and out between telephone poles and the foliage of thinly erect roadside trees.

Vic was left embarrassed and angered. And flummoxed. 'Sorry, Orla,' he said, again, as Geoff appeared in the doorway behind her, a look of sympathy and understanding on his face. 'Sorry about that, Geoff. Too much to drink, maybe. I'm going to go.'

The Sunday came and went. Vic refused to call her. Then Monday arrived and he was distracted by work, purposely leaving his phone in his locker. Out of sight. But still, by the end of the day, there was nothing from Lali, not a missed call or a text message. He became angrier as Monday evening developed but remained steadfast in his refusal to break the deadlock.

By Tuesday lunchtime he was feeling hurt to think that as easy as that she could walk away and he left school early, for a fictional dentist's appointment, to travel into Greenwich. He wanted confrontation. Wanted his say.

Standing as tall and certain as possible, he entered Rococo's with the possibility of definitive ending on his mind. Donna came to the counter.

'She's not here,' Donna began.

'When will she back?'

'I think you'd know that if she wanted you to.'

'So she's not in today?'

'No.'

'Tomorrow?' he asked. Donna looked at Vic, pofacedly. 'We had a fight. I want to talk to her,' he said.

'I'm sure you do.'

'For Christ's sake, Donna!'

'She's not here.'

He was planted on the path outside when he felt a hand on his shoulder. Aldo had come out after him. 'We haven't seen her since early Sunday, Vic. She opened up, made up the week's roster and called Donna. It happens.'

'Was she upset?'

'She looked rough. But she was okay.'

'Okay, Aldo. Thanks. When she turns up, can you tell her I was looking for her.'

Over the next two days the stated roughness of Lali's appearance and Aldo's ominous declaration that, 'It happens,' combined to complicate Vic's instinctive response to her disappearance. Gradually, concern came to outweigh anger. He left several voice messages on her phone. He texted her a dozen times. If her decision was for them to cease being, he confided to her answering service, then so be it, but he'd like to know that she was okay.

By Thursday evening he could think of nothing else but Lali, and when her phone didn't ring out but instead was interrupted by her voice, he was completely at a loss. When she spoke, it was plain and unaffected. Not her, somehow. As if somebody else had come back in her stead, armed only with her accent.

'Are you alright?' he asked.

'Of course.'

'Where've you been?'

'Away.'

'Why didn't you answer my calls?'

'I don't know, Vic. I was busy. I was away. That's the point of going away.'

'I was worried about you.'

'Well don't be.'

'Lali, are we done here?'

'I don't know, Vic. Are we?'

'What about Saturday night?'

'Didn't really work, did it?'

'And that's it?'

'I told you it wouldn't.'

'So this is it then?'

'Come over tomorrow, maybe. After work.'

'To talk? You want me to?'

'If you want to. After work.'

The near perfect equilibrium of Lali's ambivalence allowed no meaningful room for optimism. All Vic could do was amass the infinite variables of their relationship, consider the absence of uniformity in them, and conclude – Yes, she wants me, No, she doesn't. When he considered the two most glaring incidences of her unpredictability, the morning after that night in Marlowe's and Geoff's birthday, he appeared to be the sole link. It would have been reasonable to conclude that he was the problem, that there was some dissatisfaction in her with regard to him. Except that in examining both incidents, he could identify nothing that he might have done to cause them. So maybe there was something else, something he didn't know about.

With a bottle of wine placed between them, they began to talk. Lali filled the glasses on the kitchen counter but hardly spoke. There was no apology, not a trace of regret.

'So where were you?'

'I don't want to talk about that, Vic.' She took a gulp from her wine and winced as she swallowed; some cheap, supermarket Merlot.

'Well, why were you gone wherever you were gone then?'

'Vic, please.'

'What am I supposed to make of you, Lali? Disappearing like that.'

'I hardly disappeared, Vic. Sometimes I just do things. I don't always fit with what people would like me to be.'

'Is that an excuse? Ready-made for whatever else might happen?'

'I don't want to talk about it.'

'But you disappeared. For days. After we had a fight. Are those not connected? Did Orla offend you in some way?'

'Vic,' she shouted, 'it's nothing to do with your cousin. I just don't feel like talking about everything all the time.' She took another gulp of wine and placed her glass down beside his on the counter.

'Things like disappearing for days without explanation.'

'Yes.' She folded her arms.

'How can it just be ignored?'

He thought she was going to cry. Then she stepped forward and lowered her head onto his chest, collapsing into his arms. 'Please, Vic. Can we just leave it?' She turned her shoulder inward and bunched her arms up about her chest and chin as if she was freezing. His instinct was to tighten his arms around her, kiss her forehead, and promise her everything. It was irresistible, endearing rather than seductive, and he succumbed to impulse. He held her, and as he did so she slipped her hands in under his shirt, onto his bare back, and held tighter. For almost ten minutes they stood like that, and then she broke free and led him to her room. She closed the door and they fell asleep together, conjoined in tongueless repose.

Later, with darkness fallen and them both sedated, she reached out from her slumber and caught hold of his hand. Half asleep, she drew it from between his knees and brought it inside the open buttons of her top. In the palm of his hand he felt her nipple harden, and she traveled across the pillow to meet him. She tore his reservations asunder with her tongue and her thighs and her paint-chipped nails.

She was subdued then for a couple of days. Introvert and unusually careful with her words. Her polite taciturnity had a faint aura of shyness about it. But soon the old confidence returned and once again people began to feel her wrath; mainly Donna and Rococo's other staff. Some criticisms valid, others not, but the venom of her delivery was always far in excess of what could be considered reasonable.

But it wasn't directed towards Vic, so he didn't concern himself with it. The only repercussion for him was a mild embarrassment at his association with Lali that evening at Orla and Geoff's. But Orla was too polite, too sure-footed and shrewd, to charge in with irrevocable assertions. It made not for uneasy relations with Orla, but less frequent ones.

When they did meet up, Vic would ask Orla about her writing, what she was doing at a given time and how it was coming along. She would ask him about Downwood and he'd tell her the same thing every time – 'It's okay. You know. Sometimes it seems pointless, brick walls and heads-a-banging. But it's okay.' She often asked about James, who Vic knew she liked and therefore provided a template for how she might act in the event of liking someone, so proving beyond doubt that she didn't like Lali. James was James, Vic would tell her, same as always; irritable, compelling, decent, and lacking in social and moral grace.

'I think I'll write James into one of my stories one of these days,' she would say.

Then Vic would wait as awkwardly as she for the inevitable but obligatory question regarding Lali: how is she? how is Rococo's? how are you getting on? what have you been up to? we must all meet up – soon! He would answer her with grimacing favourableness, while knowing, as she did, that the answers were meaningless and the chances almost nil.

Vic's dalliance with Lali, as James still insisted it was, persisted. There were ups and downs and minor disagreements over what to do on a given evening, usually in the hungover claustrophobia of Lali and Donna's flat, but Lali's Janus-faced temperament continued to work itself in among the fibres of Vic's heart. They stumbled onward and inward.

A natural conciliator, Vic conducted his daily routines in accordance with the commitments and whims of Lali. She worked early and long on weekdays, and had every second weekend off. In the evenings she watched TV; crime dramas, sit-coms, shock documentaries about freaks and tragedies, music documentaries, and hour after hour of music video shows. She might crash out for six or seven hours at a time, after work, and just get absorbed by the flicker, and the tonal rise and plunge, of one programme after another.

While she did this, Vic prepared lessons for the following day – annotating poems, revising chapters, typing up worksheets, correcting work and keeping records. After that he would often read. Sometimes, finding it impossible to read with the glare and blare of attention deficient chart shows, he'd take a book to the bedroom and read in peace, or walk round to the pub.

About the only leisure activity they achieved consensus upon was film. Lali was an avid collector and titles were added to the library on an ongoing basis. She came back to certain films repeatedly though. Sometimes it would just be a run of scenes – a beginning, middle or end. She tended to watch them late at night, often alone; behavior that seemed both remote and intriguing to Vic.

On the evening before Vic once again became acquainted with the most disconcerting aspect of her unpredictability, they watched one together. It was Lali's choice, as usual. The only actor Vic recognized was the lead actress. Hers was a ghostly presence and the film was more about the man left behind. It had an occult quality to it, a brumous blurring of the lines between memory and reality. The main character was haunted by the loss of his lover and in the end you're left wondering what was real and what wasn't. And furthermore, did it matter whether what befell him was real or not? It was a film about grief and grieving, really, intentionally dancing on the line between stoicism and pathos. It worked on Vic long after that night, and he only saw it that once. But immediately after watching it, he wasn't as effusive as Lali would have liked. 'Yeah, decent enough,' he told her, still working it through in his mind, unready to critically commit one way or the other. Lali turned up her whole face at him, devilled by his underwhelmed reaction, and ignored him until he left.

When Vic rang her early the next morning, she told him she'd awoken in the middle of the night and couldn't get back to sleep. 'A lot to do,' she said, the flagging life of her words slipping under the low rumble of early morning business. 'Look, this bloke wants more tea here,' she said, and prompted the end of the conversation.

While Vic had initially been confounded by the randomness of Lali's moods, by her ability to take offence at almost anything, he felt that he was acclimatizing well to her. Consequently, he took her cold-shoulders less seriously, less personally. But what he found impossible to overlook was her sudden decampments. These upset him greatly, positioning him impossibly between anger and despair.

It was four days later before he saw her again. A message beeped in on his phone around seven a.m. – misst u'r call. home now. She'd missed close to twenty calls, almost five every day, and an equal amount of messages, since the morning she left for work so early. He had called in at Rococo's and phoned several times. He paid a visit to her flat but got turned away at the door by Donna. She said Lali hadn't been there for days and he didn't know if he believed her. But when Lali's text arrived on that fourth morning, its sparseness thwarted any potential for relief or joy.

She appeared withdrawn. Her hair was thickly knotted about her face and running down into her dressing gown, which was tied at the waist and crossed high and tight around her chest and neck. In her hands was a mug of coffee and on the arm of the sofa a lit cigarette rested in an ashtray, smoke wriggling upward before diffusing to invisibility.

'So where have you been this time?'

'Gail's,' came her flat reply.

'Your grandmother's?' She nodded. Her eyes were narrow and her face was melted to turmoil, and now seemed frozen there.

'Drinking together, were you?' She looked away from him, indifferently. 'What have you been doing?'

'I go to stay with her sometimes.'

'And it's definitely her you're staying with, is it?' She didn't answer. 'You can't just disappear, Lali. Then come back and expect me to be fine about it. I couldn't contact you. Nobody knew where you were.'

'My phone was off.'

'For four days? It didn't occur to you to turn it on, no?'

'No,' she said, not suggesting that she couldn't but that she wouldn't.

'What are we going to do here, Lali?' The answer was slow in coming but it came.

Vic was enormously relieved to actually meet Gail. Frequent visits to a spectral grandmother a relatively short distance across the city, coupled with communication blackouts and three or four day disappearances, had him sceptical and suspecting that fidelity was an issue he had cause to be fearful of. Gail's name had barely arose since the night he first heard it and he had long since given up hope of an introduction. He had stopped even asking about her.

Gail greeted Lali on the doorstep, her arms outspread; a tiny old lady with boundless benignity. Her grey hair was worn short and neat, and in her bantam frame there was an antiquated resilience.

'Gran, this is Vic,' she said. 'My bloke.'

And all was well with the world.

Lali raised her eyes but failed to quell the grin. She shone bright again, on the doorstep of her grandmother's house, conceding to the power of time shared. They were all a part of each other now, Vic thought. From the distant outside, he had travelled, and all of a sudden found himself on the most intimate inside. He was identified as the boyfriend, for the first time, when, in fact, now that it had transpired, he realized that somewhere in his mind he never expected to be acknowledged as such at all – ever.

'Pleased to meet you,' he said.

Gail took his hand and pulled him down to her softly wrinkled cheek, initiating him immediately, before he had time to reconsider. She held him for a moment, as if she was trying to absorb some visceral essence of him.

Everything was better for a short time after this. Lali seemed more settled, Vic felt closer to her again, and through afternoons spent at Gail's he found a homeliness that he could never have imagined possible with Lali.

* * *

Months later, and almost a year after Lali had first descended upon him, she took another unexplained turn. Perhaps it was the intimate pressure of the approaching anniversary that rattled her. Or something seasonal, maybe, he speculated afterwards. Whatever it was, he walked into it blind.

Downwood's English Department had sunk pre-dinner drinks in The Commons for a couple of hours, before sitting down to a Christmas meal in Blackheath. Vic was seated across from James. Janet Jacoby, the English Department Head, was in front of Vic and Matt Spencer, Janet's husband, was to his right. An administrative employee at the school, and meticulous and imperious foot soldier, Matt was despised by James.

57

'Why are you here exactly?' James asked.

'Why are you here?' Matt replied, pointlessly.

'Oh, would you stop,' Janet interjected. 'Partners are allowed, James. And Matt's driving. He might as well have dinner.'

'But he's not a teacher.'

'Well, if teacher is the requirement, Mr Daubin, I might question your place here too,' Matt said, full of implication.

'The breadth of my knowledge dwarfs you all, you pencil-pushing twat.'

James turned, disinterestedly, from Matt. 'Janet, I realize love and fucking have their own peculiar flights and that you're entitled to whoever you chose, but does he really have to be here? Think about it. Really?'

'Enough, James' Janet said, brusquely.

From behind a tactful silence, Vic was summoned. 'Sure,' James said, with understanding. 'But myself and Tonto here might do our growing up outside, while we're having a smoke.'

James was over it by the time he had the first drag of his cigarette. 'What a fucking twat.'

'I suppose,' Vic said.

'So where's Lali tonight?'

'Not sure. Out. Somewhere.'

'And you're still with her?'

'Of course,' Vic said.

'How long is it now?'

'A year. About that,' Vic answered.

'Fuck,' James whistled. 'I'd not have given it a week.'

'I was just thinking about it tonight,' Vic said, beginning to be irritated by James' snide but uncorroborated remarks, and trying to ignore them. 'In The Commons. That night. That date you set me up on. The night I met Lali again.'

'Wrong choice though, yeah? Should have gone with the other bird. Kicking yourself still, I bet.'

'What's your problem?'

James snuffed out his cigarette with a swivelling toe into the ground. 'No problem, Vic. Easy, mate.' He blew the last of the smoke into the air. 'Your own business. You're right.' Vic rolled his eyes, hardly mollified by the climb down. 'Anyway, we're digressing from the nub of the issue.'

'Which is?'

'Monogamy. It's a mug's game. A woman's state of well-being should be of no concern to a man. Go home with her, sure, but then you've got to pull your pants up and get back about your day.'

After the meal the whole party returned to the pub. Vic was full of fried soft noodles and chillies and he'd had enough to drink. He wanted to catch a ride out of Blackheath, to meet up with Lali. But he struggled to engineer an exit. Opportunities kept being missed as he got caught in conversations or circumvented by the swell and movement of the group. Still hoping to get away before the closing time rush for taxis, Janet collared him.

'Thanks for earlier, Vic.' He looked at her for clarification. 'For James. For taking him out for a few minutes. He needed to get it off his chest. Thanks.'

'It was nothing,' he said, rubbishing any accredited virtue with a statement of fact.

'Thanks though,' she said, again. 'So how're things with you?'

'Good,' he nodded, smiling and struggling to hear her.

'You still living in Camberwell?'

'Yeah. Spend a lot of time in Deptford though. With the girl-friend.'

'That's right, yes' she said, with a quality of polite dismissal that equaled his own. 'What's her name again? Layla?'

'Lali.'

'Oh, yes. Is she some kind of exotic goddess? Sounds like she should be.'

'She can be.' Janet laughed. 'I'm thinking I might head off home now, see if I can catch up with her actually. Just waiting for an opportunity,' he said.

'I understand completely. Just go.' She stretched to kiss him. 'Have a good weekend, Vic,' she said, licking her middle finger and dabbing his cheek. 'Lipstick. Sorry. See you Monday.'

A quick glance back, as he opened the door of the pub to leave, revealed Janet in conversation with James, him mouthing every drunken syllable with a drawling pedantry. Janet smiled at Vic, causing James to look across and wave him off with a casual flick of the wrist and a raised glass.

He stopped in at a twenty-four our supermarket on the way back from Blackheath, on a moony whim, before heading to Lali's place. Once inside the door, he put his plastic carrier bags down and took off his coat. The flat was dark and cold. He hoped to have the place comfortable and festive by the time Lali and Donna got home; new lights for the Christmas tree, large socks for hanging over the gas fireplace, and some turkey, ready-made mash potato, vegetables and gravy for dinner the following evening. When he turned on the light he saw Lali looking at him from under a throw on the sofa.

'Why are you here?'

That was how it started. With that question. Somewhere between that and hurling of the vodka bottle, she had risen to her feet with the missile in hand. It had glinted and somersaulted past his left shoulder, the acrid contents quaffing and swishing as it came through the air. Then there was a drooling thump as it hit the back of the chair and dropped anti-climactically to the cushioned seat. But her anger had not been realized without a shattering.

At first, when he saw her with the bottle, he thought she was going to come at him with it. Or down it. He moved into the room, his hand outstretched, pleading for composure. They circled each other, her asking him what right he thought he had to just barge in, who did he think he was, and just because he had a key it didn't mean that he could come and go as he pleased. And then she threw it. To hit him, he was sure. But it had missed and that incited worse.

'I was planning to surprise you. Christmas lights. Dinner for tomorrow.'

'Do I look surprised?' she fumed. 'Do I look like I need your fucking surprises?'

'What's wrong with you?'

'You. You're fucking wrong! With your condescension. And your books and your bullshit.'

'I don't actually ask you to read them.'

'You think I'm a fucking idiot.'

'I think you're fucking nuts.'

A flurry of slaps to Vic's face and shoulders, shoves to his chest, forced him backward, until he could back off no further. She took a look at the vodka bottle on the chair, but he grabbed it before she could. She was enraged, like he'd never seen her before. 'Get out of my flat!'

'You need to calm down,' he told her.

'Get out!'

'Lali! Take it easy.'

'Get out! Get out! Get out!'

'What's wrong? Tell me.'

'What's right? I'm sick of you. Sick of you tiptoeing about. Be a fucking man, would you?'

Vic lobbed the vodka bottle to her. She caught it. 'I think you need a drink,' he said, and left.

In the days after he left Lali alone with her rage, he was struck by an unexpected sense of order. Freed from the constraints of shuttling between Camberwell, work and Deptford, never sure where he'd end up each evening, he experienced a newfound calmness. No longer having to second guess Lali's moods, he found a distinct satisfaction in the mundane but uncomplicated routine of rising, working and returning home.

He managed to spend some time with his housemates, which he hadn't done in a while. There had been a time, before he met Lali, where his housemates were on the verge of being his friends.

Graham lived in the room above Vic's and his bed was as rickety as his girlfriends were loud. Urszula was tall and shapeless with slouching shoulders; a Polish-Catholic lesbian. She cried a lot. Vic liked her. They once got appallingly drunk together, on a miserable winter Tuesday, and he tried to jump her as soon as they wobbled through the door. She pushed him away with her club hands and began to cry, apologising for not liking boys. He thought nothing of it, remembering it only factually, and fell asleep across her Amazonian thighs while she petted his head and prayed for happiness.

Then there was Deon, in the large attic room. A manager at the Balham Sports and Leisure Centre, he was trying to set up his own R&B label with some of his mates from all around South London in the evenings. His colourful crew of friends dropped by at all hours. Harmlessly shifty characters, in general. Clyde was the one Vic remembered. He rattled up on their door at three in the morning. When he whistled in the letter box, 'Oi! Deon, mate. It's Clyde,' Vic couldn't ignore him. He opened the door to a hoodied and baseball-capped little man in his mid-twenties.

'Sorry to knock so late in the evening, mate, but is Deon abou'?'

'I don't know. Can't you come back in the morning?'

'No way, mate. I gotta see 'im now.'

Vic showed Clyde into the front room and kitchen area and sat him down on the sofa. He went up the two flights of stairs and knocked on Deon's door. Nothing. Still out. When he came down, Clyde was standing over the counter in the kitchen and had already cracked some eggs into a bowl. He was whisking them with a fork, and had a chopping-board, a tomato, mushrooms and a frying-pan ready to go.

'Share an omelette? I'm starvin'.' Clyde sprinkled some salt and black pepper into the egg-mix.

'He's not there. Sorry.'

'Not to worry. I'll wait. Clyde, by the way,' he said, indicating himself with an exaggerated wideboy gesture, elbows elevated and out, and hands inverted at the wrists. 'Me and Deon, we go back. He's a bruvva to me. You Vic?'

'Yeah.'

'I've heard about you. Top geezer, Deon says.'

Vic doubted this very much, but was placated by Clyde's attempts to keep him onside. Clyde rooted through a stack of CDs on the sideboard, sighing in exasperation at their music collection, before turning his attention back to his omelette. Vic was stunned by Clyde's confidence, by the crude but harmless quality of certainty he possessed.

When Clyde had served himself his omelette, and cut off a piece and placed it on a side plate, he came over and sat opposite Vic in an armchair, a glass coffee table between them. He slid the side plate over to Vic, and handed him a knife and fork.

'You wan' a drink?' he asked, quite the host.

'No, I'm okay. Thanks.'

'So, what's your game, Vic?' he asked.

'Teacher.'

'Quality! You touchy feely or old school?' he asked, but before Vic could respond, Clyde answered, telling Vic what he needed to be. 'You can't take nuffin off kids today. They need a strong 'and. Twenty lashes. Lit'racy would go through the roof. That's a fact! Numeracy? No need to worry. Kids is all into money. Business will take care of itself.'

'What do..?'

'Where you from, anyway. Funny accent. Wales?'

'Dublin.'

'Ireland?' he asked, just to be sure.

'Yeah,' Vic said. 'Southern Ireland.'

'War's tough, man. War's fucking tough. Doesn't matter what the ruck's about.'

When Clyde finished eating, he took a serviette from the pile on the table and wiped his mouth and chin. He sat back in the chair, tilted his head back slightly and gave the place the once over, side to side. 'Nice place,' he said. Then he sat up, elbows on knees and spoke to Vic, almost in a whisper. 'Listen, mate. I got a place I gotta be. When you see Deon, tell 'im I left it in the usual place. Okay?'

'Sure. No problem. I don't know when I'll see him though.'

'When you see 'im, though, yeah?' He didn't wait for confirmation. 'Sweet. Cheers for the omelette, mate.'

These began to feel like scenes from another man's life, eventually. They made him wonder how things could have been, and made him see Lali as one of life's crossroads, a crucial junction where defining choices were executed. What if he had resisted her advances? If he had continued to run the single, professional gauntlet in London, how differently might everything have turned out? But simultaneously, he realized the irreversibility of it all.

When three nights later his phone rang, he was surprised to hear Gail's voice rather than Lali's. Gail made no attempt to exaggerate or propel events toward artful dramatics, but she hung the facts out, plain and unsweetened, and allowed Vic to do the rest. Lali had arrived at her house that afternoon in disturbing form.

In the immediate minutes after the phone call Vic remained determined to keep his distance, still believing that he could detach at will.

But soon questions he knew to be undermining forced their way to the forefront. What had happened? Had Lali done or suffered physical harm? Was she filled with regret this time? Was she lying in bed wishing she hadn't said the things she said, wishing for somebody, even him, to be there for her? Had she asked Gail to ring him?

It was past ten in the evening when he arrived at Gail's.

'It's the emotional part that frightens me. I know the alcohol doesn't help, but it's how upset she gets,' Gail explained, unprompted.

'We had a fight. Over nothing really. It seemed to escalate,' he confessed.

'She kept saying your name. That's why I called.'

'She asked for me?'

'No, not quite. I wouldn't say that.'

When Lali's fits of tears had first happened, in her teens, Gail had gone in pursuit of her, chasing up the stairs after her. She had tried calming her down but Lali had just wailed louder and got more distressed. Gail learned that it was best to let her cry it out, to just listen and gently assure as Lali purged her despondency – 'What's the point? There's no sense. Why even bother? I'm tired. I'm tired. Why bother? What's the point?' A mantra of disaffection.

After that, it was days of dressing-gowned silence, sitting numbed in front of the TV. Gail fed and cared for her as best she could during these episodes, but there was never any explanation, only garbled mumbling, and crying. Nothing much comprehensible. 'Sometimes she repeats certain phrases. She cries out for people I don't know,' Gail explained, perplexed by Lali's intricate mechanics. When Lali came through the other end, she just refused to talk about what had happened. In time it was this, specifically, that Vic identified as the central failing of Lali's introversion; it lacked any redeeming qualities, like self-examination.

Vic's flight home to Dublin had already been booked for Christmas Eve and he wasn't for changing it. The day before, he called into Lali at Rococo's. Despite his visit to Gail's, he and Lali had not seen or spoken to each other in nearly two weeks.

Lali lead Vic on a walk toward the waterfront, passing the Cutty Sark; her bony masts naked and wintered, looking far too tall and too broad for her hull. The ship looked aptly seasonal, as if nature had stripped her of her cloth leafage to reveal a tree of perfect perpendiculars. They veered along the Thames Path, passed the Old Royal Naval College and pressed on toward the Trafalgar Tavern. Lali was wrapped up in a long, hooded duffel coat, just her face visible in the biting sunlight. She crossed her arms and kept her hands tucked into her armpits as she walked. She was cold and open. Clean. Whole again. Her face took on tinges of rosy red at its extremities. Shorn of her rage, she seemed penetrable.

Her sheepish vulnerability disarmed him. Without her cockiness, her aggressive surety, that was so much part of her attraction, she seemed lovable; a word he would not often have been moved to use on her. And yet it was something she was eminently capable of evoking in him. Having heard, now, the history of her, and appreciating the scope and significance of her amorphous suffering, he found that it militated against his more extreme emotional reactions – frustration and contempt.

They stopped at a bench by the Tavern. He could feel the cold through the seat of his trousers. She huddled tighter to herself as they sat with their backs to the water.

'I'm going home tomorrow. I'll be back for New Year's.'

'You have plans?' she enquired.

'Not yet.'

'Fireworks here, if you want.' She held his eyes in hers for a moment.

'Yeah, that sounds good.' Was he to kiss her, he wondered, to affirm the healing? He didn't know. 'How's Gail?'

'Great. She seems to think you're a good bloke.'

Vic tried to be unmoved. 'I've got you a present.' He took a small box, wrapped by a deftly-fingered shop assistant, from his jacket pocket. 'It's nothing much. Just thought you should have it.'

'I don't have anything for you. I've got nothing for anybody.'

'Doesn't matter. I'd bought it before . . . you know. You might as well have it.'

'Thanks,' she said, looking down at it. 'Should I open it?'

'Definitely.'

His Christmas at home was quiet. He was happier than he would have been had he not seen Lali, but was still preoccupied by thoughts of her and what would happen upon his return. So the time at home was frustratingly split between pondering the Lali dilemma at length, while at the same time trying to avoid any open conversation about her. His parents had known about her for many months, but only through a comment here and there, during brief fortnightly phone calls. They were curious and pleased. But their questions were troublesome too. Vic hadn't answers for the kinds of questions they'd have liked to ask.

'Where's she from?'

'London.'

'But the name's not English though,' his father said.

'No. It's Indian. A Hindu name, maybe. I'm not sure.'

'Sounds Indian actually, now that you say that,' his mother said.

Vic wasn't sure if the generalizations inherent in the conversation were likely to slip into racial clichés. 'Does it?'

'She isn't Muslim, is she?' his father asked. 'Not that it matters, I suppose.'

'What does she do?' his mother then asked, moving away from one of his father's hobby horses; religion, nineteenth century literature, politics and a subject generally referred to as *The English*, being his beloved quartet.

'She owns a coffee shop. Cakes, a bit of food. That sort of thing.'

'No pork though, I'd say,' his father said, trying for levity.

But Vic took it in earnest. 'She's not a Muslim, Dad. I didn't say she was.'

'That's nice, love,' his mother said, cutting across them both. 'Is she pretty?'

'Never mind any of that,' his father said, dismissing the pleasant triviality and sitting up, signaling a more serious departure. 'Now, how about that factory-line of a school you're in, how's that? How many students did you say?'

'Heading towards fifteen-hundred.'

'Ridiculous. Can't be managed. Too much anonymity.'

Vic's father was a pillar of reliability; a fiercely literate and passionate university lecturer. His father imbibed books and concepts, and found his experiences validated and enriched through the words he read all his life. His was a world filtered through an intricate mesh of literary endeavor – fiction, history, politics, science, biographies, letters, criticism and theory. They all merged into a single tome in his father's mind. Everything that happened to him could be found mirrored in something he'd read or was being explored in a volume he was trying to put together. He saw the world through literary bifocals, one part factual and the other analogous, so when he locked onto something his insights possessed the intellectual range to span generations and oceans and cultures.

Comparatively, all Vic possessed was a pair clumsy-looking, hefty-framed, notional spectacles, made of thumb-thick disinterest. He taught with empathy more than passion. He was always more like his mother, he felt; kind and patient. His parents' marriage was one of liberal decency and unassuming morality, that next to Lali's biography appeared bewilderingly mundane.

'Gail raised me,' she told Vic. 'She's been my mother. Grandmother by title, that's all.' Her true mother, Beth, absconded at the age of twenty. 'She was a drunky, Vic. That's all I know. That simple.'

Lali dismissed Beth's relevance, presenting her as a complicit player in an interminable cycle of strung out ecstasy and crippling detoxification. The Beth Lali depicted, though she surely had no real memory of her, was stubborn, destructive, apathetic – 'Gail tried to help her. She refused. Then she got pregnant. Seventeen years old – silly bitch! Too young and too stupid for anything.'

And her father? A twenty-seven year old blow-in, she told him. Washed up in North London with no known connection to anyone. Worked in the local corner-shop for a lonely widower he claimed was his brother in-law. A confusing story. Full of contradictions. 'And that man could do nothing to help find my father after he left, that's for sure,' she said.

Beth's first fall was for this charlatan. Her second was falling pregnant with Lali – all ill-advised pregnancies fall, they crash from a great height. It was as bad an idea as it looked – a disaffected seventeen year old girl with a partiality for booze and drugs and a rootless twenty-seven year old with no incentive to stay. So nobody was much surprised that when crunch time arrived, he beetled off. 'But not before taking a moment to name me – Lali,' she sighed, raising her eyes.

'But you never knew him? He never came back?'

'No. Nobody ever saw him again. I don't know if my mother ever caught up with him. Doesn't matter, does it?' she asked, with a tone of misplaced rhetoric.

Curiously, her father provoked only bewilderment in her, but never choler, as Vic would have expected. She seemed almost infatuated with his imagined memory. He evaded censure in a way her mother never could.

The first few years of Lali's life were spent in a beaten-up old pram, staring upwards at the grey skies over London's parks and playgrounds, from spring to winter, as Beth lay on grass, slouched on benches, huddled under trees, with a variety of 'drunky' friends. She hardly cared enough to even miss the man who'd left her with a child he was prepared to name but not father. She ploughed the addiction furrow, which ultimately culminated in some cocktail of barbiturates and heroin, while Lali cooed and cried, unheard or ignored. Then Beth disappeared.

'Initially, they thought she'd gone in search of my father. They heard he'd settled in Leicester and was driving a bus. I don't know from who, or if there was anything to it. But it came to nothing,' Lali explained, with self-conscious curtness.

Any hope that one day the prodigal daughter would return and heal the family wound was dashed when Beth washed up on the stones of a Brighton beach, looking like she'd been dead for years. That left Lali solely to Gail.

Lali's early school years were marked by ambition, wanting and generally being the lead performer in school dramas and choirs, while excelling at all the basics of academic education too – reading, writing, arithmetic. For a short time, she straddled high-spiritedness and scholarly enterprise. She was also pretty and forcefully popular.

The egression of more complex features of her character began around her ninth and tenth years, as the drive to be the centre of attention waned and was replaced by reluctance and taciturnity. The impressive academic potential went undeveloped and *lazy*, Gail told Vic, appeared on more than one school report, back when adjectives as revealing as that were still permitted. Lali's forceful popularity became tinged with malice and episodes of bullying bespeckled her school career. Being confronted on the issue of her vindictiveness caused her to further withdraw cooperation, and what had initially been perceived as determination in the younger child, began then to appear like nonchalance.

As Lali grew up the emergent remoteness came to express itself as rebellion. She could do anything she put her mind to, only most of what she put her mind to was juvenile. She spent a lot of time chasing boys and had a constant, interchangeable string of male acquaintances. It would have been tempting to say, 'Like mother, like daughter,' but it wasn't quite so.

Aged fifteen, she took up a number of part-time jobs in bars and local cafes, lying about her age and using her earnings to fund her socializing. A powerful capacity for industry, until then buried under general malaise, formed. Driven by the obsessive need for financial independence, she pushed any remaining hopes of academic achievement aside, in favour of hard cash, boys and nightclubs. She bulldozed through her teenage years, leaving school after her GCSEs, working and consuming hard.

Her twenties continued along the same flight-path, until she stumbled across Rococo's; a brave move for a girl with no real managerial experience and only her grandmother's equity release behind her. She made a success of it though, and it should have sutured the wounds of inadequacy and put her past in perspective.

But behind it all was an inherent combustibility. She was perpetually on edge, threatening to blow up. It was that proclivity to self-destruct that Gail neutralized. Lali was quieter, pensive, in the maternal light of Gail's probing chitchat. She grounded her, though not by any force of will.

The weekend afternoons passed together in Kentish Town, just the three of them, established a closeness. Time slowed down, it seemed, and Vic looked forward all week to the quiet ordinariness of lunches, dinners and snug idleness. But it proved to be false intimacy, both a solder and crutch, concurrently binding and illusory, because of its over-dependence on Gail.

* * *

Vic returned to London after Christmas, just as planned, and immediately set to meeting up with Lali. He needed to set them straight, he felt. Needed, somewhere in his gut, to feel her again. To fill his eyes with her and smell her. Recalling the simple beauty of Lali that last afternoon in Greenwich, he knew he wouldn't be insisting on an apology, or an explanation. He didn't know how it would all resolve itself, but he knew that all that need happen for them to begin again was for her to say, 'Yes.' To signal a willingness to do so. That would be enough for him. With that admission, he tumbled beneath innumerable images posing as memories – the illusions of her.

So on the New Year's Eve, Lali took him out to dinner, a reconciliation offering that he accepted without quarrel. They greeted the New Year with explosions of green and red and orange and pink over the Thames, lighting up Maritime Greenwich as they gazed upward, hand in hand. The past was put behind them again, where Lali always insisted they keep it.

In the February, five months after Vic had met Gail for the first time, she was gone. Peacefully, in her sleep, with no obvious cause other than age, she passed away. It was the first time he understood the term. There was none of the coercion or Old Testament intimidation that is implicit in lives that are *taken* or *lost*. Gail failed to show for Wednesday morning tea at a neighbour's, and Lali was contacted.

She went alone to Gail's, not wishing to burden anyone else. 'I make no assumptions. I don't know what anybody else feels and it's a waste of time guessing,' she said. Except that Lali's resistance to assumption was in itself an assumption. She assumed nobody cared, that nobody would want to know. Her default position beginning with the greater assumption that everyone was selfish, innately and over-ridingly self-interested to the point of negligence. She assumed, on Vic's behalf, that he'd prefer not to be bothered by the death of her dearest grandmother, surrogate mother, and only family. It felt to Vic as if something was wedging between them again. He was kept at a distance in the grieving process and it was ground he never fully recovered.

At first she appeared to be coping and although he heard her crying at night, with her back turned to him in bed, and he watched her drift off into long, absent trances as mince sizzled to charcoal in the wok, he still believed she was simply grieving.

He tried to empathize, to understand, and wanted to help, but Lali wouldn't allow enough proximity, on any level. He didn't know what happened in her mind as she lay alone at night, with all her daily distractions tripped out, and he wondered did she miss his bumbling efforts at consolation then, during those dead hours. But he wasn't allowed to know what went on inside her and so his influence was limited.

For a while, all socializing stopped and the regularity of her disappearing acts accelerated, which made little sense to him, given that she no longer had anyone to run to; what comfort could she take in an empty house? he wondered. One evening, having been unable to get in contact with her for several days, he took the

Underground to Kentish Town and rapped on the door of Gail's house, convinced Lali was sitting inside, huddled on her childhood bed, or hidden away behind the curtains of the living room. If she was, she never answered.

This series of temporary abandonments hurt him more gravely than any of her previous slights. Perhaps because he'd come to love her more, or because he appreciated the destructive potential of her loss.

But with Lali wallowing in stasis and showing no signs of being reborn into the world, he visited Donna to see was there anything they could do to help. He had underestimated the sickness of Donna's devotion, though. She was incapable of sharing anything with him, even in Lali's best interests. She shook her head, intimating that he could never understand, rebuking his attempt to breathe a modicum of civility into their uneasy acquaintance.

Between Lali and Donna, Rococo's somehow kept going and plans made before Gail's passing to open up another café in Catford got on the move again; Donna was to stay in Greenwich while Lali would take on the new project. The new project was heralded as just what Lali needed – a positive distraction. Although the initial ambition had been Lali's, the impetus for the project was now firmly Donna's. It was one of the few things Lali engaged with and it seemed that Donna's uniquely self-interested therapy was yielding modest results, until Lali changed everything for all of them.

The limits of Vic's sympathy had come close to exhaustion. Lali's self-absorption, her disregard for his concern and efforts, reeked of delinquency. He had grown increasingly impatient with her and vacillated between assertively concluding the relationship and tentatively waiting for her to return to herself. It was the closest he came to actually leaving her. Then, out of the blue, just as Vic thought he had no other option but to break from her, Lali returned to full miraculous vitality, but on the back of an entirely different project. She put Rococo's expansion on hold, deciding instead on something uncharacteristically sentimental.

Before this U-turn, when it all looked fated, and he had shaken off the initial shock of Lali's emotional stone-walling, Vic found that he wasn't as hurt by the prospect of being ejected from Lali's life as he might have expected. He had resigned himself to the end of the relationship. He was prepared for it. And he was relieved, actually. A sensation he'd experienced once before in the face of losing her. He'd had enough of her and everything that came with her. All that held him back was a certain degree of scrupulousness, unsure how soon it would be appropriate to throw in the towel on a girlfriend who'd recently lost her only family.

Then the new plan was launched. It cut Donna out without warning or consideration, and anointed him. The Catford café plan was shelved. Huddleston Road was the new plan. Lali decided what her life needed was a move, away from dreary Deptford. She sold Gail's house and used the money to finance the purchase of No. 178 Huddleston Road. What was good in her heart resided in N7.

'Vic,' she told him, 'this will be a house for us, somewhere where I feel at home. I couldn't have lived in Gail's, but I want to go back to North London.' The house was already signed for and now that she was vital again, she was happy to assume things on his behalf; her heart wouldn't have skipped a beat at this hypocrisy.

He bent to her conviction. How couldn't he? She seemed to have turned a corner and he was an intrinsic part of it. He felt responsible for his role in the realization of her plan, despite having nothing to do with its inception. He never looked back to when he figured it was all over and felt an odd relief, nor paused to consider how her skewed logic brought her to the momentous decision. North London was familiar to him too, having spent his degree years in that part of the city, and it brought him within a convenient radius of Orla and Geoff. So he was complicit. It suited him too.

But more importantly, he was back in favour. All the brilliance returned – she was captivating and exciting, and ambitious, and unattainable. It was irresistible, the opportunity to be the one that tamed the wayward soul. It was part ego and part philanthropy. Her choosing him above the business, and Donna, and everything else, elevated him. He was instilled with renewed purpose, charged with the responsibility of bringing contentment to her, and he was impatient to be the one who did so. He needed it, to validate everything he'd endured. What could salvage pride more effectively than it all working out in the end?

He packed his bags in an afternoon and paid up till the end of the month at the house in Camberwell, ready to throw his lot in with Lali. While his housemates had developed beyond the role of mere strangers, there was nothing that bound him to them.

The first months together in Huddleston Road were idyllic. The memories bolstered by the props that gradually came to populate the house. The reclining armchair, famously wrested from an antique market when they first moved in, was most obvious among them. In the subjective world of their mutual experience this story was folklore; the chair's survival of the treacherous journey home, with Lali at the wheel and him on his knees on the lowered back seats, barely holding onto the weighty bargain as it threatened, quite earnestly, to take itself and its new owner to a comical death beneath the wheels of any number of cars, and even trucks, that set themselves the task of tailgating their tiny little hatchback that afternoon.

Weekend afternoons spent picnicking on an old bed-sheet, on the dusty floor, splattered over with paint, with plastic flutes of fizzy wine and chatting expectantly about cold winter evenings indoors, were among the best times he could remember. Lali excitedly welcomed all comers – Donna, Orla and Geoff, James, some of Vic's other colleagues from Downwood, some of Rococo's staff, and other acquaintances of hers. She uncorked bottles and played tour guide through the house.

He loved being settled. Having a home. Having Lali and him together. They redecorated and furnished it. It was a place to which he was always looking to return, the first time he had known that while in London. It was all the obvious things, the clichés; turning the key in the lock at the end of a working week, dinners by the fire, surrounding himself with his own belongings and having the space to enjoy them. His happiness finally facilitated by a sense of permanence.

And she seemed happier; more gentle, her severity blunted. Vic never questioned where the severity went for that short period, whether its disappearance was wishful thinking, or whether her misery was just concealed from him. He didn't ask questions because to do so would have been to invite failure, to risk confrontation, to lose the magic of Lali.

They were properly settled in by Lali's birthday. The June heat was bleeding the city's energy by day, slowing everybody to a clammy footslog, and bringing people out into the streets at night. The evenings acquired more hours, as they seem to in summertime, and they took the Underground into Covent Garden, or walked to Hampstead, stopping in at pubs and catching buses back. On occasion, he convinced Lali that dropping into Orla and Geoff was a good idea. Geoff's birthday was never spoken of, it was just chalked-off, an aberration everyone was keen to have expunged. Orla carried on as normal, doing her best impression of herself, welcoming them both and seeing to coffees, as if nothing had ever happened.

When they returned to the house, they would stay up an hour or two more, watching TV and often having another drink before bedtime. Happy then with the extended evening, Vic would be in bed and reading no later than midnight; ten minutes reading was enough to shut down the racing mind and send him off to sleep. But Lali usually remained downstairs. It was not unlike her to still be awake a three in the morning, or to have become restless and awoken around five. In later years she would spend hours on the internet, downloading songs, reading articles or gossip on musicians, bands and actors. But back then she just watched TV and listened to music.

As early as the beginning of June, Donna had made public her plans to celebrate Lali's birthday in Rococo's. She arranged for a small celebration after closing, before heading out to a bar and nightclub. It was a plan that minimized Vic's relevance on the day itself. He didn't object. He merely adjusted his own plans.

'Where are we going?' Lali asked him.

'Dinner.'

'But where?'

'Somewhere nice.'

'Why?'

'Because Donna has hijacked the day itself, and I'd like to take you out. Just us.'

'Great,' she said. 'How nice?'

'Pretty nice.'

'What are you wearing?'

'A shirt of some description.'

They taxied to Hampstead. The vision of her stepping out onto Hampstead High Street in a sleeveless raspberry dress, flaring slightly, using his hand to support her as she stepped from the height of the black cab, became embalmed within him. Years later he could still trace the slender upward curves from the tips of her toes in her strappy heels, all the way up her silken shins and disappearing under the sateen hemline, just above the knee. Others saw it too; the taxi driver who didn't notice Vic had tipped him handsomely, the dumbfounded man in a blazer who she stopped to ask for a light, the woman climbing into her expensive car who looked Lali over, enviously, and then to Vic, and back to Lali in disbelief.

She tottered down the cobbled lane to the restaurant and they waited by the door as she finished her cigarette. When the maitre d' saw them, he came out and asked could he bring them a drink. She was nearly finished though and instead he stood out and talked for a minute, enquiring after the occasion and flirting extravagantly with her.

Dinner was in the open air, with the evening descending and the delectable but ridiculously priced wine making them immune to the decadence. Between dinner and dessert, a lavishly mascarponed and subtly rummed Tiramisu, Vic produced the birthday present. An envelope.

'Open it,' he instructed.

'Turkey?'

'I'm in over my head here. Between the dinner and present. Turkey for a week is the best I could do. The hotel is five-star though. Sun, good food, one foot in the west, one foot in the east. Loads of cultural stuff, if you like. Markets. Something different.'

She came around the table and tapped his ankle with her toe. 'Let me sit down.' A few people looked their way as Vic opened up his body and she sat down on his lap. 'Don't mind them,' she said. She returned to her seat for dessert.

Later, in the living room, she lit some candles and sifted through some CDs by the stereo while Vic went to the kitchen for more wine. He arrived back with two glasses and an open bottle.

'*Go Your Own Way?*' he asked.

'Yeah,' she said, lifting the wine from his hand and placing it beside hers. She was swaying from the shoulders and hips. Her eyes swooned and came back again as she ran a hand through her black hair. The light fell across one side of her face, accentuating her thin nose and tight drawn lips, and she moved against him. She hitched up her dress, then took his hands and pulled them down to her thighs, sliding them up toward her hips, and kissed him. By the time the next track on the album was through, he was reclined as far back on the couch as he could go, with his trousers on the floor and his shirt flung open like saloon doors. Her thighs spanned his, astride high up his lap, as she held her underwear clenched in one fist behind his ear.

Afterwards, in bed, with all the lust evaporated and the romance had, Vic was at his most content, returned to familiarity and routine with a precious memory safely in the bank. 'You know I love you,' he said. She was nearly asleep.

'I do.' She patted him on the cheek. 'Just don't ask me to marry you.'

He laughed but didn't know why.

* * *

When she told Vic she was pregnant, he did ask her to marry him.

'Oh, piss off, Vic!' she said. A baby wasn't something she'd considered. She said she wanted rid of it.

He promised he wouldn't stand in her way but pleaded with her not to be impulsive, to take the requisite time. She said she'd give it three weeks.

During that time he kept his fears to himself, though it was all he thought about. As day twenty-one passed, the units of time – days, hours, minutes and finally seconds – became agonized. He waited with an anxious expectancy for the evening she would arrive home, serenely take her seat at the kitchen table, pour herself a large vodka, and say, 'It's done.' He lived in fear of that, but he knew that if he was the one to raise the subject again it would be counterproductive; there would be accusations of emotional blackmail, and there would be conniptions and spiteful repercussions.

On day twenty-four, he awoke to find her sitting at the foot of the bed. When she heard him move, she turned and with a concessionary smile, said, 'Okay. I'll have it.'

He was fearful she might still reverse her decision, so he subdued all the rapture inside and stood up to move towards her. He kissed her and said an understated, 'Great.'

'I need to get to work,' she said, and stood up to dress.

She was six months gone, closing in on seven, by the following Christmas. Aside from the rejection of a second proposal, he remembers it for how peaceful it was. They watched some forgettable TV and Vic felt kicks from the womb for the very first time. It was then, feeling a little drunk and moved by the thrusting limbs of the imminent baby holed up in her womb, that he asked her a second time. 'I'll never marry, Vic. Not just a Morrissey song.'

Then, early in the New Year, James announced his departure from Downwood. He had handed in his notice and his decision was irreversible.

'You're welcome to come along, Vic. You know that, mate.'

'Wouldn't be great timing now,' Vic said.

Vic was disappointed to see James leave, and so suddenly, but he'd already begun to see less and less of him. After getting together with Lali, initially, everybody had mixed well enough. But as time passed, Vic and Lali saw more of each other and less of other people. When they moved into Huddleston Road that process of natural distancing moved a few steps further. By the time

James had resolved to chuck in teaching, stopped talking about it and just did it, Vic had no reasonable grounds on which to expect him to stay. He brought nothing to the table in their friendship besides the occasional pint and a chat at lunch.

After the initial uncertainty of the pregnancy, the upbeat Lali everybody had enjoyed during the first months of life back in North London reappeared, her spirit pretty much undiminished. It was another rebirth, the kind upon which Vic's perpetual hope rested; she always came back, eventually.

A room was prepared for the baby. They painted it brightly and filled it with a cot and various bits and pieces; play things and picture frames, that in the absence of anything other than a faceless projection, a dreamy vision of somebody not yet truly real, held only an abstract pleasantness. And yet these rituals filled the passing months with promise. Vic fell further in love with Lali. Her changing profile, as she expanded and slowed, endowed her with a preciousness that made her even more desirable to him; the unknown something that was as much his as hers, and grew within her, was fusing them to each other.

Jessica was born the following March and Lali shirked nothing. She tended dutifully and lovingly to Jessica; singing lullabies and nursery rhymes, cradling her and talking soothingly, changing nappies, worrying about her slightest sniffle, and buying toys and games and music that claimed to stimulate an infant's mind. He had no real cause to worry, and it was only with twenty-twenty hindsight that he came to dwell on certain small details, and wonder what had escaped his attention; what auspices of her awful act, prepared in the astringent privacy of her heart, had he missed?

Lali returned to work full-time within a couple of months of Jessica being born, but even before that she was taking calls and fretting over Donna's inability to navigate the business alone. 'I'm self-employed, Vic. What else can I do?' she said, when he suggested it might not be the best idea. 'The business will nosedive if I stay out any longer. Then what will you do?'

Financially, what she said made sense, despite the unnecessarily snide implications of her final rhetorical dig. Vic was the one with the disposable income. The nominal contribution he made to the household was used to pay utility bills, stealth taxes, and groceries, and anything that remained after that went towards Jessica's crèche. But Lali paid the mortgage. Insisted upon that responsibility.

She struggled to balance Rococo's and home and she regularly came home late, trying to make up the hours lost while readying Jessica in the mornings. They were all tired and tempers were constantly straining. Adjusting to limited sleep, at first, and then later to the demands of Jessica as she began to find her feet and her personality – from crawling, to toddling, to running, to climbing, to falling and bruising and scraping – put them at odds with each other.

And Vic struggled, too, to continue to teach in the same manner as he had before. Home consumed the majority of his energy and attention, putting work in perspective. He began to play the percentages, reducing the curriculum to core topics, flinging out the key points repeatedly, until they stuck. His teaching was less prone to fanciful fits of inspiration and more reliant on routine. Consequently, he was less exasperated and more satisfied, for a time. Until the literature by numbers, and the test scores, became meaningless, and he began to lose hope in everything.

It was when they were at each other's throats that he resorted to drawing comparisons between Lali and the Hindu Lalita, the four armed mutant goddess, for whom dissolution was considered play. He took pleasure in pointing out to Lali the sad aptness of her association with a Devi as likely to use her powers for mischief as joy – 'As neat an analogy as we were likely to come across.'

Of course, Lali, being well-versed in spiteful recriminations, would retaliate. 'And *Vic*, short for *Victor*, what's that about exactly? I think there's irony there somewhere, don't you? I mean you're the English tosser.' How she came to love that transposition, tosser for teacher; partly because it devalued him and partly because in her experience that's what they'd all been.

But the danger of fighting with Lali was that he never knew exactly what he would get. Would she bring the shutters down or would she strike ruthlessly for whatever would hurt the most? When backed into a corner, her icy quiescence could skip hotfoot to mephitic personal attacks. Confrontation with Lali was always a high-risk strategy.

At other times she presented apathetically, taking herself away for a day, more or less unannounced. Not disappearing like she had in the past, but walking out the door without warning, on a morning when she was due to leave Jessica to the crèche. On these mornings, Vic was left to ring Downwood and proffer excuses, all of which seemed to make a fool of him. The only solution he often had was to call Orla.

Lali seemed to accept the value of Orla in these circumstances, and remained reservedly cordial despite what resentments and insecurities bubbled beneath. From Jessica's first days, Orla swept down from the Hampstead hills to avert mini-drama and crisis alike. Performing duties that ranged from general babysitting to trips to the doctor, school collections, jaunts to the zoo, and organization and execution of birthday parties. She seemed intent on giving Vic and Lali the best chance possible. And she did it for Jessica as much as Vic, loving her more than she was obliged.

During those first few years, when Vic knew they needed a break, it would be Orla who offered to take Jessica. But the break he thought they needed was not the break Lali needed. An hour wouldn't have passed before Vic began to think they should get back home, but Lali would want to have that extra drink, to stay another hour, or see could Orla hold onto Jessica for the night.

Even when Orla could, and she always could, it wouldn't be long before they were fighting or sitting in silence. It didn't seem to be just Vic, or Jessica, that Lali needed to be free of; there was a void that no amount of compassion or space could fill.

There were good times too, of course. There had to have been. How else could they have sustained it? There were holidays, in Turkey, before Jessica was born but after they realized Lali was pregnant. And then Italy, when Jessica was two or three and they were all just together for a week. Lazy mornings, long walks and longer lunches, beautiful dinners, and Jessica babbling all the time in the background; an angelic white noise, melodic wallpaper in the backdrop of each memory.

But the other nights, the inauspicious nights, continued to manoeuver their way into the frame. Like the evening he returned home late after supervision at the school's annual concert. Creeping quietly in, he thought they would both be asleep, but noticed a light still on in the living room. He watched as Lali sat in the rocking chair with Jessica asleep in her arms. She was crying. Tears were swelling under her eyelids, distending the elastic skin to capacity and bursting like water-bombs down her cheek. Her face, wet, glistened in the lamplight. Some music was playing quietly on the stereo. The late-night news was finishing and the weather forecast was about to begin, but they were only pictures, no sound. He stood watching her and the longer he stood the greater the absurd sense of a mother being held by her child became; the way Jessica lay across Lali's chest, and her short, child's arm, just starting to tuck itself in under her mother's and around her waist. It was like one of those optical illusions, where your perceptual biases dictate which image you're allowed to see, and once you get stuck on the old woman, you just can't see the young girl; sleeping Jessica was holding her mother, consoling the inconsolable, trying to heal her with love.

He backed out into the hallway, towards the front door, opened and closed it, loud enough to be heard. By the time he'd hovered over the hall table, jangled his keys and hung his coat, Lali had knocked off the stereo and dried her eyes and face. The weather forecast was over. Jessica, woken by the movement, was stirring drowsily in Lali's arms, as she rose from the rocking chair to bring her to bed.

She smiled weakly as their eyes met. 'I must have fallen asleep in the chair.'

He could see that her face was blemished, the skin of her cheeks rawed by salty tears. 'Everything okay?'

'Yeah.' She kept moving past him.

He reached out and held his hand to Jessica's back. Lali stopped. 'You sure,' he asked.

'Yeah, Vic. I'm sure. I just want to get her into bed.'

He made himself a cup of tea and some toast. He was expecting Lali to return downstairs, as was her way, but she never came. She went straight to bed and was asleep by the time he got there.

Part II

He left Huddleston Road in mid-January, after almost eight years there. Moved out. That was his solution to the increasingly hostile facts of their relationship. Left his soon to be seven year-old daughter. Left Lali, conceding to the fact that love wasn't enough.

In the run up to the Christmas that immediately preceded his departure, and over that Christmas, the depths they had sunk to became unbearable. Lali no longer spoke with him. Aside from the generally poor state of their relationship, he was unaware of any specific reason for the embargo on communication that was imposed that December. He just knew that sometime around the start of the month she stopped talking to him. From there they progressed to living separately, under the same roof, with Lali taking herself to the office each night, where she listened to music or watched DVDs on the computer, or trawled the internet.

In the first few days of this silence Vic expected her to break, expected that her indignation, over whatever indiscretion he'd supposedly perpetrated, would overpower her.

After a week or so, unable to carry on in complete ignorance of each other, she began leaving him notes, communicating solely through post-its. It wasn't that she would stand in front of him and scribble something that she could sooner have said, but she would strategically place them about the place for him to find – notes about hanging out Jessica's washing, telling him she couldn't pick Jessica up from school and asking could Orla do it, alerting him to the electricity bill that needed paying.

The silence was broken on Christmas day. They opened Jessica's presents together in the morning, ate breakfast, and then took the mile and half walk to Parliament Hill in winter sunshine. Jessica's frosty breath puffed out in soft white clouds against the city's hard dysphoria, as she talked them through every turn of her wordy imaginations. With Jessica skipping ahead of them on the path, Vic and Lali's minds met on a glance, acknowledging the shared impression of Jessica's beauty; her white hat, the fleece-lined ear-flaps and their tassels dangling and jumping loosely about her ruby-red scarf, with the cold and the vibrant colours of the season embrowning her complexion. When they got home, Lali lay her down on the couch, where she snoozed, worn out by excitement and fresh air.

Then Vic and Lali made dinner together in comfortable cooper-ation; the guns of love temporarily silenced. Lali even exchanged a few words with him, among them, 'Happy Christmas.' He thought the situation was thawing out, prompting a wave of relief and the swelling of a typically pathetic affection; he never caught on, never learned to mistrust her good turns as much as her bad.

But after dinner, and no more than forty minutes of Christ-mas Day, family TV, she removed herself once more to the office. He knew then, consciously, as opposed to the bedimmed aura of dysfunction that had swamped them for years, how awful it had become. Up until then, they had been sharing the master bedroom, ignoring each other's haunting presence. On Christmas night, he relocated his sleeping quarters to the spare room. He was upset. And then came anger. Anger at her, but also with himself, for misreading her yet again, for allowing his learned scepticism to slacken.

Even Jessica, who they had fooled themselves into thinking hadn't noticed, began asking questions. She asked who was ignoring who, at one stage, and sarcastically, Vic thought. That was when the idea of moving out, of separating, first occurred to him, astonishingly. Sarcastic, he thought, what an awful thing for a still seven year-old to be.

Three weeks later he was ready to broach the subject. He put it to Lali, this prospect, his decision, in the bedroom, as she dressed. 'I'm moving out.'

Lali shrugged.

'I think Jessica's starting to be affected by this.'

'Fine,' she said, from her sitting position on the bed.

'Almost a month of silence, and this is all you've got to say – Fine!'

'I'm too tired for this, Vic. What do you want?'

'Well, I know we're not married but there's the small matter of our daughter. Do you think you might have an opinion?'

'I really don't. Move out, if that's what you want.'

'This isn't what I want, Lali! What sort of a person gets into something wanting it to end like this?'

'A masochist,' came her monotone reply.

'Do you want me to go?'

'If you think it's best for Jessie, then that's the thing to do.'

'Are you saying . . . I'm confused here, Lali. What are you saying? That me leaving is *not* what you want? Or that it *is* what you want?'

'Like you said, Vic, we're not married. If you want to go, go.'

'I asked you to marry me – twice! An out of date and irrelevant institution!'

'I agree.'

'So what are you talking about?'

'Oh, I don't know. Maybe we've needed a divorce for years, but we weren't married, so we couldn't have one.'

This was peculiar, the kind of pretentious conceptualization of a problem Vic would concoct. 'Now you're getting abstract on me,' he said, fists and jaw clenched.

'I've got to go to work, Vic.'

'I'm not giving up Jessica. I'm doing this for all our sakes. But I'm going to see her whenever I want.'

'Of course. I agree. Now, are we divorced yet? Because I need to get to work.'

There were still traces of her lethal sweep, but it was subdued. This wasn't the half of her. Her meanness had become lethargic, and without it she seemed lifeless; stripped her of her survival instinct, like an ageing boxer in the tenth round, punching out the fight on memory alone.

The months spent alone in the Highbury bedsit were the loneliest he had ever known. It was loathsome and surprising. The detestable nature of the loneliness itself caught him unawares. Although it's hard to imagine why, when the bare circumstances of living alone speak for themselves.

Just being stuck there in the evenings, counting down the minutes until he fell asleep, with the sounds of an unfamiliar neighbourhood reverberating through the door, heightened his sense of isolation; screams of girls and women – both disconcertingly playful and fearful – babies crying, and scorching sirens. Random, coarsely accented voices expanded into the long corridor outside his door and receded again, leaving nothing but the unchartered minutes of his new life as they played out against the sound of his breathing.

He couldn't focus on the TV and reading was impossible. In solitude, Lali still governed. Whatever distance from her he had achieved, there was still all that she possessed of him that couldn't be returned – the years, the kindness, the dignity. And then Jessica, too. Jessica seemed to him the whole of them, a child born of anything virtuous that had ever passed between them. She was the love and the compassion; everything else was decay. And Lali now withheld her, just like she had withheld herself all those years. He wanted to hate Lali, to cut the malignancy of her from his heart, but there were just too many pounds of her in there.

'I could die here tonight, in this room,' he wrote in his journal, which he had erratically begun to keep again, 'and nobody would ever know.' The school might ring his phone when he didn't turn up for work, he thought, but when they got no answer, how would they find him? He imagined stumbling and clipping his head off the side of a counter, or the TV stand, with his phone out of reach.

Lying paralyzed and speechless, but conscious, from a Friday till God knows when – two days and three nights, anyway. It would be Monday before he was missed, but how many hours or days would inch past before anybody would find him crumpled on the warped linoleum floor?

He couldn't sit in alone and he couldn't think of anybody he could call. He was too embarrassed to ring Orla and Geoff and ask could he stay with them. 'Of course. But why?' they would be bound to ask. And what then? What could he have said then? Could he really have explained, as if it wasn't embarrassing for them all, 'Oh, you now, just because I – a grown man, a father, responsible for a beautiful daughter, and of steady middle-class profession – feel lonely.' Could he have humiliated himself before his extended family with his abject failure to navigate adulthood alone, as we're supposed?

He couldn't escape his irresolvable feelings for Lali. He tried walking the streets under the pretence of needing milk or bread, and taking Underground rides to places he'd never been. He tried the cinema, alone, an extravagance he had sweet memories of, but found that he couldn't make sense of the pictures. All he could think of was what time it would be when he got back to the bed-sit. Would he be able to sleep? How could he shut Lali out? How would he fill tomorrow evening, and then the weekend?

The bleak nights had defeated him within a working week, and he started down a road he would have deemed pathetic only a year before – fraternizing with Downwood's younger members of staff, trying to reinvent himself in the role of hardened socializer. He began living vicariously through the lives of his still truly young colleagues, with their tales of drunkenness and lust. It was his only sanctuary from himself and his thoughts of her.

The drinking with his younger colleagues was heavy and sporadic at first, until the sporadic flurries of consumption became copious and frequent; everyday at the train station a quick pint turned into a knees-up, followed in time by a glass of wine at dinner – microwaved noodles – which then, over an alarming short span of time, turned into a bottle and an hour or two down at the roughneck local.

The benefit of being stark-raving drunk upon home time was that he slept, straight through and almost immediately. Without thought. Without memory. Lay down and sunk unconscious with just a busy blackness thrumming in his brain. But then morning came and it was the same old performance all over again – no work prepared, no food in the fridge, no long dark hair to be brushed, or lunch to be prepared. Inevitably, mistakes followed.

The foundations of regret, however, were laid before his exit from Huddleston Road. The portents of intimate failure began with Janet Jacoby. Janet, for reasons he was unaware of and declined to enquire after during their briefest of interludes, pursued him, although his attempts at fending her off were effete. Feeble resistances.

His initial encounter with Janet was unsavoury, effectively adulterous, beginning not after he and Lali separated, but before. One miserable rainy night, after a ridiculously late parent-teacher meeting the previous November, followed by a few winding-down drinks, they found themselves alone at last orders. With her Matt away and Lali at home in foul mood, Vic fell into Janet's marital bed. She confided in him that she'd always kind of liked the idea, as she rested her head against his ribs and slapped his lank penis over and back against the skin on his lower abdomen. 'What, playing with my cock?' he responded, concretely, only partly aware that he wasn't sounding much like himself.

He could have offered explanations – the painful disintegration of his primary relationship, his family's imminent fracture, sadness, frustration, and the nausea of lovelessness – but they would all have sounded excusatory.

Then his relationship with Lali broke down and he left for Highbury. The undignified fizzling out of him and Lali coincided with a particularly grueling few weeks of inspections from Her Majesty's Inspectorate, during which all Downwood's staff had felt the strain. On another evening in the pub, celebrating the end of the HMIs forensic autopsy, Vic found that Janet landed with increasing regularity beside him, the more drunk she became. While Matt dined on Pringles and talked shop with other, more decorous, members of staff, Janet came to say her amorous good-byes. She put her arm around Vic, and leaning down towards the low stool, she whispered, 'I'm so sorry to hear about you and Lali. I'll come visit you during the week. We'll have dinner and talk.' With what seemed like nothing left to protect, he saw no reason not to submit to her obliging charms again. It was easy to do, and a distraction from his abject circumstances.

Janet's visit meant he came back to his bedsit early. She brought Indian and two bottles of wine. He knew he shouldn't, but he showed her in. He never asked where she was supposed to be at seven o'clock on a weekday evening and who might miss her. That was her problem. She sighed at the sight of the bedsit – so bare, so dated, so unlived in.

It was no more than a small sofa, a TV and some pieces of cheap cutlery bought from a discount store – two of the forks were already bent out of shape after he tried forking potatoes. The sleeping area, though she never made it that far on this visit, was much the same – a thinly partitioned cupboard-room, no room for anything but a bed. He was sleeping in a sleeping-bag and using some balled-up, old T-shirts for pillows.

They shed their clothes with a resigned reticence – this is what they'd become – and went about it with guilty detachment. In the living room, with her bent over the back of the sofa. He just followed her lead. He accepted what was offered. Gratefully, hungrily. But he neither seduced nor procured.

On her second visit, she arrived with a vibrant green and yellow throw for his ragged sofa – a little too late to be making it respectable, he thought – and a duvet, bed sheet, pillows and covers for the bed she had yet to visit. This time Vic provided the food and the wine. Again, he asked no questions of where she ought to have been or where she thought it might be going. Of course, he knew where it wasn't going. But he ignored any opportunities to address the prognosticating illness that was invisibly present in their affair.

Later, as she sat on the edge of the newly dressed bed, pulling her high boot onto her foot, and zipping it up to her knee, one leg sitting suggestively across the other, dressed only to her skirt and bra, with her shoulder length hair falling forward and tickling her clavicle, and the comeliness of her pearled earlobe in his eye, he felt a seeping. She was nearly gone, and he was still there, boxed-in, in that room. She was off home to a husband who would probably embrace her warmly and kiss her as she came through the door, and talk to her in bed as she drifted off to sleep. Vic wasn't prepared to lie alone in the darkness, kept awake by the permeating menace of Lali that invigilated over the close of every day, so he began to dress too.

'What are you doing?' Janet asked.

'Getting dressed.'

'Have you got something to do? It's late,' she said, looking at her watch. 'Why don't you stay in bed now?'

'Can't sleep.'

'So what are you going to do?'

'I need a drink. I'm going to go out for a bit.'

'And maybe pick up some girl, maybe?' she said.

For the first time, the casual illicitness of them took on a semblance of being more than they had both been pretending.

'I don't think I'm going to get into this one, Jan.'

'I thought we had a nice time.'

'It's got nothing to do with you. I'm just looking for a drink.'

'But if there was something else on offer, when you get out there, you'd consider it? Right?' she said, rational in tone, though her agitated hands betrayed her.

'I don't know,' he said, honestly. 'Maybe. But it would just be because I don't want to be here. It's about this place and all the other stuff. It's not you.'

'Isn't it?' She straightened herself out. 'Who are you kidding, Vic?'

She went cold on him for a few weeks after that, until the afternoon he was leaving for Dublin, for his living mother's funeral. It was an unfeeling end to what felt like a squalid affair, the vacant heartlessness of which seemed to be a decent metaphor for how badly his temperament had been disfigured. He didn't blame Lali for this aspect of his behavior, or the debasing facts of a life lived alone, but it was what happened, he supposed, when you got involved with the fucked-up – eventually, they fucked you up too.

With the distraction of Janet extinguished, Vic spent a week scouring Islington in search of a bar that might pass for a local. Somewhere he could go and be recognized, but not known. Eventually, he settled on an Irish pub in Archway, not for its homeliness but because as his walking legs grew stronger – after weeks of trying to out-walk what he carried in his heart and mind – and the exertion less demanding, Lali's voice grew louder. Only bustle, density of bodies, and sufficient drink, could silence her. So he stopped in at The Harp one night and claimed a barstool for himself. It was good enough, he felt, his expectations being so pitiful by then, and he soon clocked-up enough hours at the bar so as to achieve virtual invisibility; just another broken Irishman in a London bar, on the run from something or someone, no different to those who had gone before him. Thoughts of Lali and Jessica pursued him to the ends of each night, and so he drowned and swallowed them.

Then, one weekday evening, he got caught up in the atmosphere of a European Championship qualifier. For an hour and a half Lali faded into the background as he downed a few pints and got embroiled in the tension of a 1-1 draw. He felt part of something, and any kind of kinship was worthwhile at the time. Floating on the froth of belonging, he watched, buoyed by the strange collective viscerality of sport; the intimate crowd, the ritual atrophies of hope and despair.

The Harp's patrons swallowed their nerves in composite gulps every time the Bulgarian's got over the halfway line, hands over their faces every time the Bulgarians swung in some wickedly dipping corner, all European and graceful and technically superior, and cheering manically when the traditional big lump of an Irish centre-forward bundled the ball, and two cultured Bulgarian defenders with it, into the net, equalizing gloriously late in the second half, and so confirming what the partisan patrons of the pub thought all along – these classy European footballers, they're a bit soft! A little under the influence, Vic set his mind on the vital next game, a must win against the Welsh, in Dublin.

When James then unexpectedly rose from the embers of his self-imposed exile, after years, the decision was finalized. 'My Celtic Cousin,' James began, as he was prone to doing when Vic's commitment to a venture was required, or when he was back-peddling upon realizing he'd gone too far. His roving eye had fallen, too, upon the Ireland-Wales game, then only two weeks away.

Vic hadn't heard much from James since he disappeared into Asia on a one-way ticket. But he had often imagined him, in the midst of fraught domestic times with Lali, reclined on a hammock, slung between two coconut trees, on a long lost beach in Ko Pha Ngan, with some unilingual, indigenous beauty nestled in beside him, enjoying the uninterrupted sound of his own lecture, pondering a half-constructed postcard to him: apologizing for Lali, and trying to entice Vic towards a new start in a place with no rules. The last Vic had heard was from Thailand, several years before, but this email, he assumed, had emanated from somewhere much closer. It hardly mattered though, and he gave it no more thought. He was uplifted by the prospect of an evening with James in Dublin. It was as if nothing had changed, the fraternal tone and boldness of James' words. Vic responded immediately. The plan was formalized. Flights were booked.

In the interim, Vic made a fist at keeping in contact with Jessica and in a broken and confused way tried also to maintain relations with Lali. He wanted to see more of Jessica but it became apparent quite soon after leaving that he couldn't just be swinging by every evening and taking her out. The rationing of his time with her left him feeling victimized.

Some Saturdays he brought Jessica to the cinema and although she seemed to enjoy it, he dropped her home feeling as if the time had been squandered. There was a shopping trip too – some shoes for her and a lunch. When they returned that Saturday with Jessica's new shoes, Lali answered the door still in a dressing gown, still looking hungover. For the first time since Vic had known her, she looked older. As if time had crept up on her; dry skin and drooling, grey ridges sagging beneath her eyes. Even her hair looked undernourished, brittle to the touch. He followed her into the kitchen while Jessica played in the living room.

'Are those shoes okay?' he asked.

'They look okay, yeah.'

'Is there anything else she needs?'

'No.'

She didn't make an issue of Vic's attempts to help out with Jessica, she just ignored them. It wasn't a principled stand on the matter either, it was that she couldn't be bothered.

'Lali,' he said, and reached out to place his hand on her arm. She quailed away from it. 'Let me help.' She said nothing. 'She's my daughter too. Let me help. What else does she need? There must be something.'

'There isn't.'

'I miss her. I just want to be able to do something for her.'

When Lali looked up there were tears in her eyes that she would not let fall. 'I know,' she said. It was concessionary and not without feeling. Like she wanted Vic but couldn't allow it. And Vic knew then, despite the raggedness he'd noted on the doorstep, that if she wanted, she could have him back. If she just smiled, the wrinkles would fall away from her face and his misgivings would disperse.

'Are you okay?' She had finished her coffee and looked suddenly impatient. She'd shown him too much already. 'Are you okay?' he asked again.

''Yeah.'

'I'd like to see her during the week sometime. When I get a better place. Nicer. Maybe she could stay over.' Lali nodded her head and left her empty mug down at the sink. She stood then, purposefully withdrawn, and waited. 'Okay. I'll let myself out then,' Vic was forced to conclude, in exasperation.

He went into the hallway, calling out to Jessica. She came running from the living room and flung her arms around him, in the usual way, as he knelt down. The ungraspable vulnerability of Lali cranked and heaved heavily around them, searing through the cavernous air like a whistling radiator pipe. Every part of Lali was calling out, except her voice. That she wanted him then, needed him, seemed irrefutable and tragic.

* * *

He left London under a cloud, although his was not the only cloud looming on the North London skyline that week. But he couldn't have appreciated that those mushroomed puffs, flowering upward from innocuous cumuli over the course of months, were poised to move in on them like a raging supercell. He may have been too preoccupied with himself to notice. He'd stripped himself down to the bare minimum by then – sleeping when he could, breathing because he had to.

In general, since he'd left the family home and Jessica – everything worth anything gones – he'd lived in a punitive manner. There were no monkish tonsures, but he'd shaved his head entirely, cutting away part of himself, tearing his identity asunder, in self-disgust. He had submitted to the pain of humiliation, marked himself out as scarred; redemption through asceticism. An inherent, cultural predisposition to self-abuse.

The sparseness of his appearance was mirrored in his habits, a punishing denial of life's basics – food, water, laughter. Although, in certain areas, when it came to that other kind of drink, for example, his Spartan devotion inverted; suffering through endurance and excess.

On the Tuesday morning, as he prepared to get free of London for a few days, there had been the phone call. Jessica insisted on calling him, despite Lali's equal insistence that there was no time before school.

'Yes, of course I'll be there. It's your birthday.'

'You missed the last one.'

'What?' I did not. Last year? No. No way, I was definitely there, Jess.'

'No, Mum's birthday.'

They had fought the morning of Lali's last birthday and Vic had remained late at school, in a sulk, marking copies and tidying his classroom.

Lali had snapped at him over breakfast and he had bitten back. But Lali always had to ratchet up the intensity. She didn't like the challenge and with Jessica within earshot, she stood up at the table and seethed, 'You're such a little bitch sometimes, Vic! You know that?'

She dressed and left for work without a word, and he retaliated by skipping her birthday dinner with Jessica and Donna.

'Vic?' Lali was on the line; to scold him, to warn him.

'Yeah?'

'Don't let her down, Vic.'

'When do I let her down?'

'When you're angry with me. Just be here, Vic. For her. It's nothing to do with *us*.'

'*Our* daughter is nothing to do with *us*? Is that one from your quack boyfriend's couch?' Vic had recently been made aware that Lali had some random bloke stay over, only weeks after he'd left. She dismissed it as none of his business, but did allow herself to tell him he was a psychotherapist. Vic's own indiscretions prevented him from any measure of feigned self-righteousness, but it didn't make him any more capable of equanimity.

'Vic, I really can't be bothered with this. Just be here.'

'How about you send her to me for her birthday? How about that? Maybe I can't be bothered.'

'Fine. If you can't be bothered about your daughter's birthday, then there's nothing I can do.'

'Oh, I'm bothered about her, Lali. Believe me. Jessie matters.'

'And I don't. I know that. But unlike you, Vic, I've always known. What's that word of yours, the one you like to throw about – *transient*. Everything is transient.'

'No, Lali. Everything is not transient. Some things endure. They reach outward. Some people are balanced, Lali. They can relate to people beyond fucking and fighting.'

'I've got to get her to school, Vic. Just be here.'

The line went dead and he threw the phone to the floor. He pulled his sock up over his heel, beyond the toes it had been dangling from as he sat only partly dressed for the duration of the call, and slipped his foot into his work shoes. Then he stood up and straightened his trousers, tucked in his shirt and went in search of his bag and coat. First period – covering Year 12 history. No worksheets or instruction left by the absent teacher and nothing prepared. Bollocks. He'd wing it, do something he was familiar with, but not English. Stick to history, the lesson they were waiting for and a variation for him, he thought. The American War of Independence. That would do it. Then Dublin. A change of scenery.

Dressed, it occurred to him that he was starving. But he didn't know whether he wanted to gorge himself or just leave the hunger to fester, keeping him on edge, making him crabby; sometimes his bad moods disinclined the mouthy South London students to act up, made the lessons run smoother – teaching through fear, or threat, just like it used to be. Of course, it was equally possible that one of them would arrive to school unfed for longer than him, or having been beaten around the back of the thighs with a coat-hanger, like a kid from a Lou Reed song, ready to match his short-temper with genuine aggression, with rage straight from the urban underbelly.

No breakfast, he thought. I'm bloated enough as it is. He was late, looking at his watch and wondering how he was going to cross the city, north to south, in forty-one minutes when the journey, including walking time and assuming all was running to schedule, was a minimum of fifty.

'So, the War of Independence was as much about taxes, unfair English taxes, in the eyes of the *Americans*, descendants of the Puritan English driven from England, as it was an ideological opposition to England and its monarchy. There were also factors of land, and raw materials for industry to be fought for, a European market to be protected, but basically it was the taxes that . . . the so-called Americans,' he said, and looked out at the blank expressions before him; expressions of disinterest and confusion, twisted and shaped onto a collage of spotty-faced teenagers.

'Sir?' a voice asked.

They used not listen at all as he spoke. They carried on as if he wasn't there – plain ignored him. So he began to stand silent at the top of the class as they talked, often shouting obscenities at each other. Anger and volume were defunct instruments in lives like these, he learned

'Yes, Sam? A question?'

'I'm going on my holidays, right. In summer, innit. And what part of Ireland you from?'

By lunchtime he had presided over four lessons, none of them particularly inspiring. Just text and talk, the barest advancement on chalk and talk; alliteration for rhyme, teaching for the teacher regardless of the student – easier, and altogether more self-satisfying. Had James still been on-staff he would have been chuffed.

In the staffroom, he made for what still was referred to as the smoking room, where all the interesting teachers used to hang out on their breaks. It had held tenaciously to its worn moniker but was now a place of withering memories, a room where many of the faces Vic had begun teaching with years before were still to be seen, except they were jaded now, by the profession and by the slow draining-off of time. The workplace smoking ban had merely served to lift the smog that slightly obscured this fact, the fallen beauty of their quixotic youth. It left Vic with a feeling teetering on the brink of disgust. When he looked at their bored expressions, knowing that however far from grace they had fallen that he'd crashed through the floor of it, he wondered about the point of education.

When the bell rang for the end of the day and his vocational charade came to an end, he clasped his hands and sent the Year 9s home without homework.

Heathrow was crowded, as expected. Unpleasant, but thankfully busy. He arrived at the airport two hours early, having gone directly from work, as if he couldn't stand an unnecessary minute more in a place that was haplessly associated with his misery. He hardly needed much encouragement then to fall into a maudlin state, but the cool beer provoked just such a hollow nostalgia.

Apart from the quenching sensation, what struck him was his wordlessness. All those people buzzing around, literally thousands, within arm's reach, and not a word spoken. A few people who leaned over him at the bar apologized or joked, or dropped open-ended statements into the air. But he failed to engage. He just thanked or apologized accordingly, and went back about his wordlessness. The morning's phonecall meandered in and out of focus, merging with a plethora of other incidents, and began assimilating itself in his narrative of uncomplicated ruin.

It was only as he sat on the Aircoach, staring out the window onto miles of motorway, ugly developments, then city streets, and finally suburbs, that his body finally unclenched, sensations returning as he began to uncoil. His shoulders and neck, even his thighs, rolled out in some measure of fleshy anaesthesia; sleepily relaxed. He voluntarily, not like a yawn, stretched his jaw open wide, swiveled it from side to side, and felt the skin around his eyes and forehead shifting across the boney plates of his cranium. His face broke its solemn mould. His eyes opened wide and seemed to glare, although they were only looking. At nothing, just shapes as they flickered by the window of the insistent coach, persevering through the traffic.

As he disembarked onto the tarmacked terminal area, just outside the hotel, he looked around, it only then occurring to him that he would need a taxi. There were two waiting. He stood motionless as the coach driver unloaded the suitcases and rucksacks onto the path. One passenger after another picked up their bags and made their respective ways to waiting cars, the hotel reception, or the taxi rank. He waited, his bag at his feet, as an elderly couple took the first of the waiting taxis. The second taxi was there but another man breezed in ahead of him. A third taxi pulled up, but once again he declined to move toward it. Instead, he walked up the steps and into the hotel bar. He wasn't meeting anybody and he wasn't really sure yet where he planned to go.

After an hour at the bar, he had a headache of Lali. The rarified thorns of family decay had begun to break through their cerebral hide, and beneath the unforgiving light of the hotel bar, the piercing inner wounds now surfaced in bruised pools of blood just beneath the skin. His face, with its ashen eye-sockets and pale lips, and his bowed spine, were outward indications of the rot that had set in – a blight of the soul. In search of a quiet distraction from his predicament, hours to kill and no strength for words, he booked himself a room and headed for the restaurant. He ordered a meal and a bottle of red wine.

By eleven o'clock that night he was in a taxi, more unable to be alone than he was reluctant to speak. Within fifteen minutes, he was in the sitting room of the family home, having gate-crashed his parents' peaceful retirement. It looked identical to how it had been when he was a child, except for the new windows, put in a few years before.

They were dressed for bed by the time he arrived, dressing gowns and slippers, with half-drunk cups of tea at the ready. His father was in his armchair and his mother was curled up on the sofa, defiantly alive. The fire smouldered. Everything seemed at ease, safe and calm.

His arrival meant that his mother rushed out to make a pot of tea. His father looked up and spoke kindly.

'So what brings you home?'

'Just here a night or two. For the game tomorrow.'

'What game?'

'Wales. Crucial qualifier. Couldn't be missing that.'

'Oh, right. Who're you going with?'

'A Welsh fella. I used to teach with him.'

'And what about school? It's not mid-term over there, is it?'

'No. I've taken a few days. I told them I had a funeral.'

'Who died?'

'Mum.'

'Oh, right. That sounds serious,' his father said. 'We'd better tell her to rest up and forget about the tea.'

'I just needed a break. With all this stuff going on.'

'And how are they?'

'Jessie's fine. Or she seems fine when I see her.'

'And Lali?' his mother asked, arriving back with the tea.

'Who cares?'

'Vic, I don't think that girl is well,' his mother said, sympathetically.

'She's fine. She's just nasty, that's all.'

'She should see somebody.'

'She's got that covered, as far as I know,' Vic said, condemning her further with unsubstantiated implication.

'Maybe it's for the best.' His father's reservations had never been openly declared but were no less clear for having only been intimated.

'Not for me, it isn't. I hardly see Jessie. How's that for the best?'

'Well, I don't know what to say then. If we say it's a pity, you accuse us of sympathizing with her, and if we say it's all for the best, you accuse us of not knowing anything about anything. Which is it?' his father put to him.

'What happened, Vic? Is there any hope here, for Jessie's sake?' his mother asked.

'We're done, Mum. That's all I know.'

'But what happened?' she asked.

'*She* happened,' Vic said.

Although he could think about little else, discussing Lali with his father and mother was not possible. It was too painful to see their disappointment at the mess he'd made of himself. He felt humiliated by his failure to see the dangers of Lali, and in their sympathetic manner, straining to understand as much as actually understanding, more was done to condemn him than any criticism. He evaded talk of her, wherever possible, because from whatever angle he approached her, it was insufferable. And when his parents observed his discomfort in discussing her, and changed the subject to Jessica, not realizing that Vic's shame in failing to provide properly for her, to give her the stability, unity, and a model of functionality, it was even worse.

With the fuss of his arrival subsided, he sat down quietly in the smaller and less comfortable armchair. He had a cup of tea followed by a whiskey. His father had one too. They drank slowly as the heat of the fire lapped over them.

He had fully intended to stay at the hotel. But once home, there was no reason to leave. It was like getting wrapped up in an impenetrable warmth, with his troubles kept at bay. He slept on a creaking camp bed, a makeshift attempt at hospitality, placed in the domestic dumping ground that used to be his bedroom. It felt like being sixteen again, but without the luxury of hope. If Vic had known when he was sixteen what life would be like at thirty-five, he'd never have surrendered his humble room in the family home.

With pains in his back, and an unexplained bruise on his upper arm – those inner wounds scarring outwards – he took himself down for some breakfast. His mother was waiting, not surprised then as she had been the previous night.

'Sausages? Eggs?'

'No, Mum. Thanks.'

'Juice?'

'No, it's okay, Mum,' he protested. He knew his mother's over-compensation was his fault, for landing in on top of her unannounced. He knew what she wanted was to have everything ready for him – breakfast, lunch, and dinner – and that had he given them adequate warning, or any warning, that he certainly wouldn't have spent the night on a decrepit old camp bed.

After breakfast he excused himself and made his way back to the hotel. He occupied himself by showering and putting on clean clothes. Then he lay on the bed for a few hours watching TV – morning chat shows, gardening and property programmes, the odd news bulletin. It was a calm cyclonic centre, where Lali seemed further away than she'd been in a long time; her hard insistence muffled.

Downstairs in the bar, he ordered some tea and a club sandwich. He folded a newspaper neatly across his knee and began working his way through the rainforest of articles and pullouts on the big game against the Welsh. He contentedly sipped his tea and launched into the sandwich, scattering crumbs onto the paper and into his lap.

Not once in the entirety of the afternoon did he think of work or consider too deeply what it would mean to be found out. He didn't care. He was so relieved by the temporary muting of Lali that he thought he might even have liked the idea of being found out. Certainly, the thought of throwing his hat at the whole show, his life in London, was ever-present. He felt sure that had there been no Jessica he'd have acrimoniously resigned from Downwood many years before and walked away from London. And there lay the irony; he was bound to his misery by what he loved the most. Jessica meant that he had to see it through. He had to go right to the end of it. There were no shortcuts. He had to stick around and become more deeply steeped in Lali's bilious influence.

Towards late afternoon he took a taxi to Lansdowne Road, stopping in for a couple of pints in Jury's. He had read just about every article on the game available in print that day, and had little left to distract him as he sat in the packed bar. He didn't want to thumb through pages of politics or editorials, all that was left to read by then. He sought no distraction from the game, for fear the panacea of relief would evaporate the moment he looked away. So he drank slowly and kept his head down.

Then, bang on time, James was standing beside him; oddly, for a man so averse to responsibility, James placed great emphasis on punctuality. Although, true to his inscrutable nature, his regard for punctuality applied only to matters that were of importance to himself; a man of subjective principle.

Vic stood up and was embraced enthusiastically. Through James' heavy coat, dusty and pilled, Vic felt his bones. He had thinned, like hair, about the torso and legs. Still distinctively himself, just less of him. His face was creased, turned in on itself all across its troubled surface. A face of seamy witness; pale and flaky, grizzly stubble with slight tinge of grey about the chin, and a woollen hat pulled down over his ears and onto his eyebrows. His coat, pulled tight around his chest, framed his poignant spirit, as if it was all that held him together. 'You Irish bastard,' he said, winning a few uneasy looks from those around them.

He took off his coat and hung it over the back of Vic's stool, squeezing in bar-side, as Vic took his seat again. James' clothes were clean but faded; a long-sleeved T-shirt under a short-sleeved one, a pair of loose-fitting jeans and some cheap, beaten-up trainers. The double layers did nothing to obscure his gaunt upper body and there were sharp edges and jutting joints and limbs pushing through the clothing.

'You've lost a bit of weight, have you?' Vic asked.

'Have I?' he said, looking himself over. 'You all set for a beating then?'

'You want a drink or have you had enough already?'

The conversation was still on football as they left the bar. Once outside, they were distracted as they negotiated the crowd and the barriers, the calls for sale or purchase of tickets from touts, and by vendors selling match programs and fast-food.

'I'm surprised you're still in London, Vic. I thought you'd have left by now. Never suited you,' James said.

When he then asked how everything was, Vic knew that the afternoon's moratorium on Lali had expired. He tried to downplay Lali's demonstrable influence by citing Jessica, but it failed to shift the focus of the conversation.

'That's a strange one, I can tell you. Lali settling and mothering. How is she? Still a fucking time-bomb, yeah?'

'I suppose.'

'And all is sweet with you two, is it?'

'Not really, no.' Vic paused, not knowing how best to confirm for James what he had always thought. 'I moved out a few months back.'

'Fuck me – you lasted that long! Top marks for effort, mate.' Vic shrugged. 'And what about the kid, who gets that?'

'She's with Lali,' Vic replied, stolidly.

'And Downwood? All the old crew still there?' James asked.

'More or less. Staff turnover not as rapid as it used to be. Janet's still the Head of English. Still with Matt,' Vic said, and suddenly felt he had strayed where he had no right. 'But what about you? Where are you living?'

'Here. In Dublin, my friend. Where better? I figured if you were anything to go by, I'd probably get on alright.'

'I hope this match is good.'

'No bother if it isn't,' James said, and put his arm around Vic's shoulder. 'We'll leave and go drinking.'

They stood up suddenly, on eighty-one minutes, and clambered over the legs towards the aisle. They were ignored, other than when they couldn't be because they were blocking somebody's view. Nobody in the stadium lifted their eyes from the game, from that historic potato patch that the FAI passed off as a football pitch. Even the stewards looked on, oblivious to their duties, with the game winding down to a dull 0-0, a result equally useless to both teams, with barely ten minutes to go.

Vic had had enough. James didn't seem pushed either way. They were out of the stadium and in a taxi, heading for the city, before the final whistle had blown.

The traffic was alleviated by the crowds still crammed into the city's pubs and bars. As they passed through Ballsbridge, a few green jerseyed supporters began staggering through the doors for a smoke. The match was officially over. 'Fucking beautiful,' James said, admiring the determined joy of a bare-chested, robustly paunched man with a tricolour pouring down his bulky back, and a cigarette dangling from his mouth, both arms raised in the air, fists closed, forearms tattooed, and staring defiantly out at the passing cars.

As they came towards Merrion Square, Vic called for the taxi to stop. He paid up and they began walking towards Grafton Street. Suddenly, the thought of changing his flight and just going back to London seemed the only thing to do. The end of the match seemed to bring an organic end to his sojourn. All he was doing now was waiting, hanging around for a flight when an earlier one was possible. Some new impetus had him impatient to confront his problems. To face Lali. To force her to love him, maybe. Or if not, to hurt her back, to really do her over. To gut her. Not with the punch-pulling sneeriness to which he'd restricted himself so far, but with all the gall he'd been suppressing.

When he proposed this aloud, James urged him to sit down and think it over. 'Why not just hang on for the night and go back in the morning, as planned,' he reasoned. What was to be gained by leaving half a day ahead of schedule? What would he do when he got there, back to his Highbury hell? What was the difference really, whether Vic went then or in the morning? 'You're hardly hardly going to turn up for work, are you?'

When they reached College Green they crossed back over the road and continued towards O'Connell Street. Traffic seemed to have grown heavier and Dublin became just like any other city again – highly strung, self-important, aggressive, with time at a premium.

Their dinner turned out to be a hamburger from a chip-shop on Dorset Street. It was consumed on the street, the seepage of fumes and grime a destitute blanket around them. The grease of the burger vomited over the powdery lip of the bun. Vic sucked the flavoured greasy dropping from his finger and wiped his hand on his trousers, as he chewed the last of it.

'What do you want to do?' he asked James.

'A drink. Another drink. Definitely.'

'Maybe I should go.' Vic knew he needed to stop but his hand reached into the air to hail a taxi, even as he was admitting to himself that hitting the airport wasn't going to help. A taxi swung in, up to the kerb.

'Ease up, Vic. What're you doing?'

'I think I need to go home.'

'You need to slow down, mate. Come on. Have a drink. We'll find a pub.'

Vic pulled down his arm, as if it had shot up in an involuntary spasm, and mouthed an unintelligible apology to the taxi driver, pointing to his watch, and the ATM at the corner, and miming a phone call – a host of bogus excuses – before the taxi driver had even wound down his window. The driver mouthed something back that Vic had no trouble understanding, and pulled back out into the traffic in his urban tank, cutting across a learner driver in a small car.

They entered the doorway of Brooke's, the first pub they came across. The place was wedged, people shoved and pushed wherever they'd fit.

'What's going on, Vic? You're very edgy all of a sudden,' James said, as the pints settled on the bar.

'I just feel the need to go. To move.'

'Back to Highbury by yourself? What then? Why don't you hang around a while. We'll catch up. Tie up loose ends.'

'I need to ring home,' Vic said, and took his phone outside.

There was no answer, at the house or on Lali's mobile. He rang again, half an hour later, and then again shortly after that. Still there was no answer. He wanted to talk with Jessica. He felt alone and distant. He needed to hear Jessica. And, inexplicably, he felt he needed to hear Lali.

After several hours of drinking and talking with James, he finally relaxed. He accepted that there would be no return to London before his scheduled flight in the morning.

It was after midnight when they arrived back at James' room. A plastic garden table was pushed up against the wall, littered with empty tins, old newspapers, a couple of discarded teabags in a disused ashtray, and a pile of books; an anthology of modern poetry, chunky-looking Greek philosophies, Durkheim, Camus.

The fixture for the ceiling light was bulbless. On the patterned and worn carpet, by James' mattress, was a small collection of spirits and a few stray cans of beer, empty and crushed. James leaned down and the switch for the electric heater clicked on, its bars lighting up.

'Pick a weapon,' James said, pointing to the bottles on the floor.

Vic chose the whiskey.

James took a glass from the sink and rinsed it for Vic. Then he took another, unrinsed, and lay down on his mattress, fully clothed and still in his hat and coat, and pulled the blankets up over him. 'There's a spare one on the shelf,' he said, pointing just behind Vic.

'No, no,' Vic said, waving the offer away. 'I'm fine. I'll just leave my coat on till the place warms up a bit.' He took a seat at the table.

'Yeah,' James laughed, tipping whiskey into his glass. He took a mighty, slurping mouthful from it to make sure he didn't lose any as he leaned back against the wall. 'Nice place, eh?'

Vic had begun to notice a slurring in his own words and drank more slowly, but James continued to swallow his drinks in vast gulps and refill with uncompromising intent. He filled Vic in on his lost years and they came again to know each other. They slipped into familiar discussions, re-tracing the steps of common interest, finding their groove, as old friends will.

'Tell me, Vic,' James implored, eventually, 'what's the story with Lali? Indulge me.'

Vic didn't feel ready for it though. It was too direct and James knew too much for Vic to protect himself. 'How come no novels?' he asked, as diversion, glancing at James' collection of books on the table. 'Aren't they your staple?'

'Not anymore. They're acts of hope, Vic. Negotiations with the stochastic. Naked artifice, trying to impose order where there isn't any. Willful denials of reason. Worse than religion: an inbred impulse of the pre-psychological world, before we became conscious of consciousness. I can't get through them anymore. They're archaic, really. Now, how about Lali?'

'It's over. I told you,' he replied, futilely.

James paused. 'It's been good seeing you again, Vic. But I'd be inclined to be worried about you. I thought, maybe, that as I slipped a few drinks into you, that you'd open up.'

'I've been open.'

'Then tell me. I can't remember when I last heard a good yarn about a man and his woman.'

'There's not much to tell. She's a lunatic.'

'All love is lunacy.'

'But this is unhealthy lunacy. Look at me. Invented the death of my mother to come and watch a football match. Sitting here. Drinking straight fucking whiskey! And I'm still talking about her.'

'Except you're not. You've barely mentioned her.'

'Well, it feels like she's all I talk about. I can't get away from her.'

'You want to?'

'I've got to. She's nuts.' In the momentary lull, Vic was suddenly prompted to ask the question that had never been answered to his satisfaction. 'What do *you* know about Lali, James? You obviously know things I don't.'

'Not much, I'd say.'

'But some.'

'A little.'

'Just tell me, James.'

'What do you want to know?'

'How you know her?'

'It's unimportant, Vic. But she was sleeping with another friend of mine. You know that. Long time back.'

'Spell it out, James. What did she do?'

'He thought it was more than it was, that's all. She wasn't what he thought she was.'

'So she slept with somebody else. So what? Happens all the time. Presumably it happens to most people until they find the person they stay with.'

'Then she fucked a good friend of his.'

'Who was you, I take it.'

'Yes, that was me.'

'And that's what your objections have always been about? I don't understand.'

'I'd never inflict myself upon anybody, Vic. I hoped that she'd be decent enough to do the same. Or that she'd spare people I knew, at least.'

'Did you love her?'

'Fuck, no!'

'Did she do a number on you?'

'Vic,' he said, breaking for a moment from his dispassion. 'You know me better than that, my friend. I knew what I was doing.'

'And your friend?'

'We're not so friendly anymore. Naturally.'

'But you can't blame her entirely. You knew what you were doing.'

'I don't blame her. I don't blame anyone. It was a decision I made. A bad one, in hindsight. But nobody died, as they say.'

'So why were you so against the idea of me and her?'

'Because I like you, Vic. And I knew things about the woman you were getting involved with and I couldn't see how you could survive it. When you first asked about her, I thought you were just after a casual thing, or that she'd chew you up and you'd get the message. But you wouldn't back off. She'd got in under you.'

'And why not tell me all this? Why didn't you tell me back then?'

'You wouldn't have listened. And it's not too flattering either, is it?'

'Since when did that concern you?'

'You see, Vic, even this, this conversation. You're so fucking naïve. Nobody is immune from the opinions of their peers. You're lucky to be standing at all.'

'I'm no angel myself.'

'No, Vic, but you're innately good.'

'I don't know about that.'

'I do. I'm telling you, too much time is wasted on mitigating contexts for people who would be better off dead.'

The hardness of James' words was arresting. It was a sudden and unexpected shove, two-handed and muscular with foreboding. It urged Vic to go no further. Told him not to pursue James' story, to keep to his own.

'What was it you saw in her then? What was it that you believed I wasn't able for?'

'She's a myth, Vic. All girls like that are. Your desire for her is rooted in some unattainable fantasy. You think you can save her. But once you get close to people like that, you begin to lose yourself. You just spend all your time chasing them, pandering to them, getting rejected and mistreated, only to be welcomed back when it suits. And they destroy people like you. And it's not even their fault. It's your own, because you've let them. It's not a very romantic thing to say, Vic, but you can choose who to love. If you must have it, this *love*, it must be a negotiation. Otherwise it's just servitude, on one level or another.'

'James, it's too late for this. I'm already knee-deep.'

'You're too wound up to see what I'm saying. She's going to swallow you up. You've got to find a new way to negotiate her. Not with her, but the experience of her.'

They talked a little more but James spoke less and less, the conversation coming gradually to a close. James' energy disseminated, over the course of minutes, it seemed, and then his eyelids slipped slowly closed. Vic waited but when James failed to speak again, he moved quietly towards him, through the shadows, and lifted the glass from his hand and placed it on the floor. James' sleeve was rolled up around his elbow. Vic took the extra blanket from the corner of the room and folded it over him, up to his chest, under his chin, as he slouched back against the wall. He stretched over him to flick the switch on the small radio, to keep him company.

As he did so, he heard something break and crackle under his foot. He could make out shards of broken glass, or plastic, on the floor, but it was too dark to see.

As a flamenco trumpet from the radio soared and jarred, a cool blue complement for the warming orange lambency of James' heater, Vic closed over the door, leaving James to his breathless sleep, among empty glasses and bottles, and the crackle of an old transistor radio.

Beyond the murky shelter of the room, Vic came out onto the walkway of the third floor. The wind had risen and the rain was driving across the courtyard. A shallow but deepening pool of comingling puddles could be seen as the besmirched light from the lampposts around the courtyard shimmered and feinted across the surface. The apocalyptic husk of a burnt-out car, with one door swung open, that he'd noticed as they came in, made him feel threatened. The blackened stairwell, climbing down from the third floor, was a solid case, with all the lights along the way either broken or missing. Damp and cold, and dirt, he thought, were what he smelled, as he stepped carefully through the darkness, unable even to see the graffiti that was surely scrawled across the walls.

It was quiet until he came to the first floor. When the wind calmed, the sheets of rain could be heard lashing forcefully onto the ground at the bottom of the stairwell. He bounded down the steps, trusting his instincts to find something underfoot, and ran out of the flats onto the street.

Drenched and freezing, he reached a taxi rank. Two taxis sat idle. He knocked on the window of the first one. The driver looked startled. Vic dripped almost as much water in his lowered window as was powering onto the windscreen from the sky.

Back at the hotel, Vic peeled off his soaked trousers and socks, hung his coat over the radiator in the bathroom, and turned on the shower. He was still shivering uncontrollably when he got out, so he dried himself off, put on a pair of dry socks, and climbed into the bed. He wasn't sober and he couldn't sleep for the cold. It had wrinkled his skin and given his customarily wan complexion a sickly milkiness. He lay still under the duvet, everything clenched, until the comfort of the bed began to defrost him, and he finally fell to sleep.

Despite his late night, Vic was at the breakfast table by half past nine. After breakfast, he took himself and his bags to the lobby and crumbled into a tub chair that looked onto the forecourt through an expansive glass front. The previous night's storm had passed but a weak wind continued to fence and parry with the flaccid trees of early spring. It carried a diaphanous spray of rain against the glass, speckling it with crystalline pimples, as he read the newspaper and waited for the next Aircoach to pull in.

Within twenty minutes the coach was pulling out, a few hours too early for his flight, and he was on his way back to London. He stared out the window of the coach, remembering Jessica's present and putting a reminder into his phone. He decided to avoid Highbury for as long as possible and resolved instead to go straight to Jessica's party. Then he texted Lali to tell her he was on his way to the airport and would be back to see Jessica by evening.

The flight was rough – inner turbulence rather than atmospheric – and Vic only just held himself together. He concentrated hard on the footsteps of the stewardess as she strolled up and down the aisle. A man next to him said a few words as he sat down, and Vic was much relieved when he managed to respond without breaking into a sweat.

He couldn't listen to anything and he definitely couldn't read. This, he remembered thinking, arbitrarily enough, was another great difference between himself and his father, whom he had not yet called since leaving their house on Wednesday morning. Vic's father recovered from hangovers by retiring to his bed for the afternoon, with a newspaper or an arcane Eighteenth Century novel, whereas Vic lowered the blackout blinds and implored sleep to take him. Given Vic's fragility in this respect, it was amazing, frankly, that his attendance at Downwood had been as good as it had over that particular academic year. He had come to admire in his father everything he felt was lacking in himself – discipline, self-knowledge, real intelligence, passion for things beyond himself.

What Vic wanted that afternoon on the plane, more than anything, was a blacked-out room and silence. He'd have settled for the hypnotic hum of activity somewhere in the background, luring him into an in-flight snooze. But he didn't get it and the cramped short-haul aircraft didn't help any.

In London, the weather was changeable, a little colder than Dublin but brighter. As he turned the corner onto Huddleston Road, he saw Lali's mid-sized hatchback parked lopsided outside the house, one front wheel up on the curb and the back two sustaining equilibrium. From the distance of the corner it looked as though she'd hit the curbside tree.

On the front step, he rang the doorbell but there was no answer. He dropped his sports bag to the ground and rooted through it, hoping to find his keys. He was allowed keys, just in case of emergencies, or if an appliance needed turning off; Lali was forever leaving ovens on or taps running.

There was a quietness, but he made little of it, reasonably surmising that Lali must have taken Jessica for some kind of extra birthday treat. He closed the door and kicked his bag in against the wall by the coat-stand; another old relic salvaged years before.

In the living room, he flaked out on the couch, stretching the length of it. The weight of fatigue began to work on him. He momentarily considered going up to their old bed, just to piss Lali off, but the thought alone was enough to satisfy him. He closed his eyes, hoping for a few minutes respite before they all came through the door, but he was unable to sleep in the cool, still air.

He sat up and scanned the cluttered coffee-table: magazines; a side-plate covered in whole-wheat granules and a crusty dollop of butter scraped onto the rim; weeks old sections of weekend newspapers; a fluorescent pink hairbrush; and big clump of Jessica's hair, balled-up beside the brush; a nail-scissors and file; and finally, what he was looking for – the remote control for the TV.

He soon became irritated by the TV, though, and went to the kitchen, where he cut himself a slice of cheese; the only edible thing available. Then he poured a glass of water and decided to distract himself with the internet.

Toppled on the stairs was a bottle of vodka, lid off and empty bar a few insignificant dribbles lolling in a shallow pool, as it lay on its side. His head cocked agitatedly to the side, his shallow-dished ears like satellites feeling for a signal, an audio clue. But still nothing. Just a dust-settled oppression. He had felt it as soon as he opened the front door. A strangeness. Although he hadn't taken it for injurious straight away.

He called out but by then he knew he was in need of a miracle. He stood up onto the first step, already with a fair idea where the domestic orienteering would lead him. It was visions of Jessica bursting through the door, back from wherever she was, and being confronted by a brutal reality, that prompted movement, where otherwise he may have been incapacitated.

He found Lali, not as he expected – just covered in vomit and her own shit – but worse. In the small box-room on the second floor that they used as an office, where they kept their computer and a random collection of his books, she was floating, lifeless, in the middle of the room.

The computer was still on and was churning out a single track relentlessly, volume low and on repeat. He stepped urgently over the upended chair, and closed down the music library with a scuttle of the mouse and a punch of his finger. He kicked an empty, plastic phial and it spun across the floor.

A moronic panic swept over him then and he rushed toward her and tried to lift her body upward, free of the choking tension, as if she might still be saved. He had some absurd notion, something gleaned from a gritty western maybe, of being able to take her down and lay her out, and restore her. There was something indescribably unnatural about it; *her* suspended in the air like that, unfeasibly still, bulging purple in the face, tongue out, waiting – how long? – to be found.

He swayed beneath Lali's insensate physicality, his arms clasped around her lower thighs, propping her up. But it achieved nothing, as her head and torso slumped rigidly to the side, like a slackened puppet, her deadweight continuing to cause the cable to yank at her throat. An indeterminate span of time passed before he was able to pry open his arms and free himself from the gestures uselessness. He phoned Orla.

'Where's Jessie?'

'Here, with us. What's wrong?' she asked.

'What about her party?'

'Lali phoned this morning. I took care of it. Vic, what's wrong?

'Come quick. Please. It's Lali. Don't bring Jessie.'

After that sparsely sentenced exchange, he glissaded downstairs, oddly unaware of his feet, and opened the front door. It was the end of afternoon and the light was fading fast. He sat down on the step.

When Orla arrived, she encouraged him into the living room. He sat and listened as voices came and went. He answered questions from paramedics and police as best he could and with as few words as possible. He listened until the only voice left was Orla's, making calls and fielding them; his parents, Donna, and of course to Geoff, who was at home in Hampstead, trying his best to conceal from Jessica the awful truth that was kicking its heels, cruel with patience, around the next corner.

It was nearly midnight by the time the last policemen left and the ambulance had pulled away onto Tufnell Park Road with Lali, her lacerated neck, and bruised-blue face, rattling rigidly about on a stretcher, as a paramedic, sat hunched over her, respectfully and professionally sullen.

* * *

Lali had been so forthrightly anti-religious that it was impossible to know how to acknowledge her demise. Having been privy to her vigorous resistance to collective sensibility, it seemed to Vic that it would have been disrespectful to mark the end of her life with any form of religious service. And demonstrating respect was important to him, not because he thought she deserved it, but because he thought that in rising above it all, he might salvage something.

When consensus was reached, it was for a civic cremation. And it rained all the day, as if she was affronted by the thought that people had gathered in her memory, by the inescapable ritual overtones of any such occasion; an ironic hissy fit from beyond mortality, he snorted, that really would have summed up her crazy logic.

He was cognizant of little on the day but the teeming rain, the way it came down over the cemetery and crematorium in East Finchley. There were multitudes around him, the familiar, the half-known, and the largely unknown. As he retreated to a grassy area to the rear of the mourners, a significant but disparate gathering, the ground beneath his feet and his shoes became his focus. Had ever he looked at his feet more than during those hours? Ever paid more attention to grass? It didn't crunch or scratch like summer grass, it was more like wet elastic – slippery, pleasingly soft. It collapsed under his weight and sprawled outward, like a crushed

134

many-legged insect, the green legs reaching out and clawing upward from beneath his onerous soles.

Beyond his toes, his gaze was drawn to the steady trickle of rainwater pouring earthward, down from the dome of the umbrella held above his head by someone unremembered. Then he returned his attention to the rarely-worn shoes – shiny-like-new and brown leather. It's unlikely he would even have noticed them had he not spent the day with his eyes on his feet, wary of another stranger subjecting him to their well-intentioned but useless pity, or the awful discomfort of the umteenth family member bereft of the necessary words.

They were shoes bought for a previous occasion; bought *for* him, by Lali. *Her* shoes had defined her, on a daily basis. They told you how she was feeling; the extent of her happiness somehow proportional to the height and slenderness of her heels. In fact, over the years her shoes had proved probably the only reliable barometer for her moods. Stilettos meant sheer delight. To his mind, the appeal of a good heel lay in the associative memory of Lali gushing with sexy confidence and mischief, rather than the elongated, graceful potency it infuses into an otherwise ordinary pair of ankles and calves. This entirely subjective fetish was one of the more benign aspects of Lali's legacy.

But it was the aesthetic incongruence of his one-hundred and twenty pound shoes, four-hundred-plus pound suit, and the mud and grass that it was all sinking into, that made them so singularly remarkable. The formality of funeral dress seemed absurd to him in that moment. Surely death, of all occasions, attested most convincingly to the irrelevance of the superficial. What an utterly odd thing to do for the dead, he thought; to dress-up.

The only physical sensation he was aware of was Jessica. She was a weight at the end of his arm. A pulse, a constant, steady reminder why he couldn't just close his eyes and leave it at that. Their hands swung. Intermittently, she tugged at his hand and he felt it in the shoulder. Sometimes she pressed her cold cheek to the back of his hand and he felt her tears roll between his knuckles, into the crevices of their gripped support. Jessica's was the pain he felt. For himself, there was nothing.

Jessica didn't care what he felt, of course. His feelings were as irrelevant to Jessica as Lali's reasons; all that mattered was whether he was there for her or not. And no matter what misery he allowed himself, he just couldn't knowingly leave with Jessica holding on at the end of his arm. That, he said, was what marked him apart from Lali.

Had she been there, of course, she have would retorted. She would have said, 'Yes, Vic, but you would never want to be anywhere other than here,' suggesting to him that his easy contentment betrayed an inherent lack of ambition. It meant he could never hope to understand her inner demons, her irresolvable conflict between self and obligation. They couldn't cohabitate and one couldn't consciously be chosen over the other. Indecision and utter frustration strangled her, is perhaps what he would tell Jessica, when she was old enough. If she wanted to know.

As people began to leave, he sat with his tie loosened but still around his neck. He had yet another glass of wine in his hands. He'd been drinking red wine for days without ever feeling drunk. Jessica was upstairs, passed out from emotive exhaustion, in her good clothes.

His father had come in, patted and clasped his shoulder, heavy and sincere, and his mother held his face and kissed him, uttering some indecipherable words, before they left for Hampstead where they were staying with Orla. A few of Vic's colleagues glanced into the living room as they passed down towards the door, and offered commiserative smiles. He nodded in recognition of a shared sentiment but had nothing to add.

After the initial shock of discovering Lali on that hideous March evening, he swung unpredictably between rage and turgid paralysis. Both of them empty, hollow sensations. Then, after a few days, he settled numbly in the broad domain of the latter, in what felt like an analeptic trance.

He was able to converse and eat, modestly, but it was only with Jessica that he could raise himself from this hebetude, smothering her in his fearful arms, constantly affirming his presence and seeking assurances from her that she was coping. Her overt mourning, the tears and tantrums of a child, amplified over the following weeks, gradually decreased in frequency but didn't quite stop. They came and went, but never seemed complete.

There was no language that could adequately evoke the depth of feeling Jessica caused in him. And it was not only in the absence of Lali that this sentimentality welled up and swelled out. When Lali had been pregnant, he'd secretly wished for a girl, and it seemed then that he could bring any of his dreams to fruition just by wishing hard enough; with ear pressed to Lali's peachy belly, he'd whisper, 'How's my girl?' And he could see her in his mind, even then, the way she turned out to be. Was that possible? Doctors and scientists, people of procedure and method and reason, would say – No. But he swore that when he had an ear resting on Lali's wonderful bulbous tummy, while she sat cross-legged and arched backwards on the couch, he was capable of envisaging Jessica, somehow able to see her in all her different stages of beauty, one ephemeral vision after another, blended together, yet distinct; what she was, and what she'd become.

In the days that followed Lali's death, he worried constantly about Jessica. Her silences became more worrisome than her tears, with her disturbed but wordless sleep being worst of all. Her night-time tumultuousness aroused great unease in him. He was unable to disregard what he knew to be commonplace; Jessica had always been an obstreperous sleeper. He watched over her some nights, reading too much into facial twitches, imagining there to be a nameless desperation in the way she licked her lips and swallowed when her open mouth left her parched. Like her mother, her long hair, though Jessica's was considerably fairer than Lali's lustrous pitch, did not stay swept back for long. She rolled and kicked out, and turned, so that the hair ended up splashed across her face from the back of her scalp. Often, while whipping through her hair with a brush, he would unreasonably put it to her that she must try to sleep more peacefully, with less commotion.

It was not the knots themselves, of course, it was the disturbed sleep. The painful knots were portentous and remindful; he worried that in sleep, Lali's demons chased her too. He worried that no matter what he did, he could never protect Jessica from something darkly genetic.

* * *

He tore himself off the couch, where he'd taken to falling asleep in the weeks after returning to Huddleston Road. He downed a pint of water and rinsed away the dryness of the previous evening's bottle of wine. Orla was doing the school run and was expected shortly. She had volunteered to help out with Jessica for as long as was needed.

'Juice?' he asked, readying breakfast.

'Yes, please,' Jessica said, shrugging sleepily.

'Anything else, love?'

'Waffles,' she said.

She was sitting at the table, swinging her legs, crossed at the ankles, not fully awake. Her hair, as usual, a tangled mess and her pyjamas creased. The kitchen was shaded from the bright April morning. She looked to be shivering a little in the coolness.

'Why don't you go and throw on your dressing gown. You look cold.'

She slid wearily off her chair and moped out of the kitchen. He turned on the radio and dropped her waffles into the toaster. Hanging over the clothes-horse was Jessica's un-ironed uniform; one of the previous night's jobs that never got done. He pulled the ironing-board out from the coatroom under the stairwell and plugged in the iron. Pressing the sleeve of her jumper to his cheek, he felt the dampness.

When Jessica arrived back and sat down to her waffles, promptly delivered to the table and set beside her juice, he finished ironing her skirt and shirt.

'Do I have to go to school, Dad?'

'Absolutely.'

'Why?'

'Loads of reasons,' he told her. 'Education for one – it relies on regular attendance. To see your friends, for another.'

'Don't you have to go to school?'

Vic had not yet returned to work and his employers, through sensitivity or uncertainty, made no attempt to push him in that direction. When he said he needed more time, everybody knew it was a bad idea. Even Jessica knew it was a bad idea. When she asked, one evening, how he had got on at school and he told her he wasn't ready for work yet, she told him that she wasn't ready yet either, but Orla had said, 'Getting back to normal was the best way of getting back to normal.' He had begun to feel that going back to where everybody knew him, and what had happened, back to uncomfortable commiserations and a familiar environment now rendered unfamiliar by pity and discomfiture, was something he could easily do without altogether.

At the sink, he stood considering the cleanliness of the counter and draining board. Lali had always left a chaos of crumbs, spillage and crockery behind her in the mornings. There was a part of him that had always imagined how much simpler his life would be without her. Now that she was gone, he found that day to day life was indeed less fraught, but what his fantasy hadn't accounted for was the silence, and how freely her presence would roam in it.

He was weighing up the significance – perhaps the insignificance, the irrelevance – of this unaccountable memory of Lali that had descended upon him, staring out the window at a menacing crow squawking from the roof of their small garden shed, when a horn beeped outside. Jessica was still sitting at the table playing with half a waffle, pushing it through a mayonnaise sludge, still in her pyjamas and dressing gown, her ironed and slightly damp uniform draped over the ironing board.

'Orla's here, Jessie. Come on, we need to step on it. Put your uniform on, wash your hands, brush your teeth – all that stuff. As quick as you can.'

He went to the front door, opened it, and waved. Orla understood and she turned off the engine and got out of the car.

Having apologized for running a little late, and Orla having assured him that it wasn't a problem, Jessica arrived in the kitchen – shirt buttoned up perfectly, shoes and socks all good, but skirt on back to front. She handed Vic the hairbrush as she explained to Orla's questioning expression the problem of the difficult button at the top of the skirt. He began tearing through her hair with the brush, realising that even though he was surely hurting her, Jessica wouldn't make a sound.

Orla reached out for the brush, suggesting to Vic that he might go and ready himself. Then she pulled Jessica's head protectively to her midriff and began fixing her skirt.

When Vic arrived back down, Jessica's skirt and jumper were neatly folded over a radiator and Jessica and Orla were propped up on the couch, watching the morning news. Jessica in her pants and pyjama top, with an open book on her lap, and Orla rubbing her upper arm as if to warm her.

'The skirt was a little damp,' Orla said.

'I thought the ironing fixed it up,' he explained. 'I made her lunch though. It's in the fridge.'

'Good, I'll make sure we pack that up before we go. You get off now. We'll be fine.'

'They're not expecting me in today. I'm going to . . . you know. I'll be around anyway. You can head off, actually. If you want. I can bring Jessie to school.'

'It's okay, Vic, I'll bring her. We agreed. And it's best to get some kind of routine going, for the both of you. You do whatever you're doing. Today.'

'That would be good. Thanks.'

'Vic?'

'Yeah?'

'Take today, by all means. But you should really think about ringing Downwood and telling them when to expect you back. They may be calling in supply day to day. You might even go back tomorrow. You need to go back.'

'I need time.'

'How long, Vic?'

'When I'm ready.' Jessica began to shift uneasily under Orla's arm. 'Look, I know I'll have to go back. And I will. When I'm ready.'

The numbed trance he had been surviving in since the cremation had begun to subside. Anger now filled the void, and on the back of this he set about cleansing his everyday world of Lali's memory. He hadn't slept a night in the bedroom since it happened. He started there, whipping off the bed sheets and the pillow cases and throwing them out. Binned. He looted the wardrobes and packed four bin liners full of her clothes and shoes into the attic.

He'd have thrown them too, but he wondered if Jessica would ask where they went and leave him having to explain. He cleared her bedside table of everything bar the lamp. The inventory of the discarded included: a few post-its with scribbled messages and one minute drawing of a stick man and woman beside a house – probably done one morning when Jessica crawled into bed alongside her hungover mother; a single studded earring; a couple of magazines; several receipts; and some make-up stained baby-wipes. He opened the blinds and the window and let in some light and fresh air. He swept the floorboards and then hoovered. He decided he'd buy new bedclothes and felt satisfied with the erasing of Lali's wight from at least one room. A stray and pleasing thought of bedding some stranger in the newly clothed bed then crossed his mind, and he looked forward to it, envisaging it as the final, euphonious act in the exorcism of Lali from the master bedroom.

Emboldened by his initiative, after weeks of sluggish and slavish nothingness, he unlocked the door to the office. It was virtually untouched since he'd last been there. The emergency services, a paramedic or a policeman, had taken down the wiring cable and taken it away, but the rest was as he had found it that afternoon.

He picked up the overturned chair and sat down, vaguely aware of the macabre connotations of now putting Lali's fateful prop to mundane use, but also aware that once he started down that road there would be no end to it. Would he not drink from her mug or sit in her seat either?

He swiveled from side to side on the chair. He felt the wheels under him slip a little on the laminate floor, and for an awful instant the thought occurred to him, Did she not actually intend to do it? Maybe the chair, on its wheels, had slipped, and her morbid game had tread a step further than she ever intended. All sorts of confliction surged from within until he calmed himself down. Look, he instructed himself: noose tied to beam; head placed in noose; standing on chair. What else, other than finality, could have been the objective? Stop trying to redeem her now, he admonished himself. Simply follow the trajectory of the facts.

He was not anywhere in the vicinity of even-tempered acceptance, of forgiveness.

The computer was still powered up, on standby. He clicked, then double-clicked and the homepage opened up. Then he began tidying around the desktop, scooping up five or six pens and placing them in the mug he used for a pen holder. He tore up an old bank statement and put it in the bin. A pile of papers, printed off and accumulated over months, was on his right. He placed it on his lap. Pulling the wastepaper bin over towards him with his feet, he began discarding the pages: leaflets for Portuguese hotels; a draft letter to Islington Council that was never sent, complaining about unfinished roadworks at the end of the street; a story printed from Lali's Hotmail account about a girl who shared a bed with her python; old worksheets and comparative grids he'd made up for *Of Mice and Men*; a list of London glaziers. And then the poem.

It caught his attention because he had no recollection of printing any poem, and Lali, of all kinds of literature, was most contemptuous of the pretensions of poetry. It was nine lines long, and forty-four words from beginning to end, entitled, *Murder for Me.* The title, as trite as it sounded, like something from a TV detective series, was unsurpassable. The title seemed mesmerically significant.

Many minutes passed before he could clamber over those three words and explore further what it was he'd found. Obviously, he was instantly aware that it was a poem, with its alignment and stanzas and irregular line length, but for several minutes it was the bold imprinted title that held his attention. What precisely he read in that first instant, he couldn't be certain – was it *Murder For Me*, or *Murder of Me*, or *Murder Me*? – but it took abrasive hold of him.

That Lali had printed a poem was strange enough to begin with – odd enough to have made him sit up and suspect something wasn't quite right, even without the contextually stunning title – but that she had held onto it, knowing what fun he might have had at her expense, was unfathomable. Once he had pried himself away from the title, he glanced down to see if the poem was accredited to anybody. He wondered had Lali been secretly penning poems, and for a moment felt excited by that thought – discovering a hoard of unrealized material, a body of work that might appease the ill-will her memory was dripping in. Just for a second, the question, Was this destined to be a ground-breaking episode in contemporary literature, the moment where Lali ceased being the dead mother of his child, and where they, he and Jessica, became the surviving lover and daughter of a tortured poet? crossed his mind. It elevated him, for an instant, this deluded idea of a troubled artistic soul as an explanation.

But there was no poet. No name. It was then he moved into the body of the poem – nine lines, forty-four words. The words were nothing like genius. They were aspirationally melodramatic. There was an air of desperation, but it seemed to him that the over-reaching effort of trying to make drama out of nothing was where it originated. There was a hint of pain, he supposed, but it was overplayed. How could these words mean anything to anyone? Why were they worth printing? The title seemed about the most impressive part of the whole lyrical failure. But Lali, who rarely read anything other than music magazines, and was derisive of the humble contribution to the literary world he made through teaching, and of his 'sniffy' interest in reading – two, maybe three, novels a year, maximum – had found in herself the need to save this paltry piece of chopped-up prose, pseudo-poetry at best, it having made such a significant impression on her. And yet there it was.

He must have read it twenty times while sitting in that swiveling, office chair. Then he took it down to the living room and placed it on the coffee table. He watched it, as if it were some deceptively inanimate object scheduled to leap into action sometime soon, or some insolent pupil whose response to sternest reprimand was being awaited. But it didn't budge. It just lay there, obstinately mute despite everything Vic knew about it, despite the fact that he'd caught it red-handed and saw through its pretensions of profundity. He didn't know exactly what it had done, but he knew for sure it was involved.

From there, he moved to that old chair of his, via the kitchen and the fridge, and sat with a beer in hand; it was early, still morning. He put his feet on the footstool and looked at the poem that now rested in his lap. Seriously, he thought, as he glanced toward the walnut cremation urn on the mantelpiece, How could you have bought into this shit? He read it again, several more times. He knew literally what it was saying, and conceptually he understood it too – this wasn't Yeats. But it was so pedestrian in its wretched-ness, completely predictable in its melancholy. It was the kind of stream of consciousness tat he might have turned out himself during his adolescence.

How could this poem have meant anything to her? Where did she get it? Who wrote it? He had already scanned quickly through her files to see if there was anything else to be found, but it came to nothing. Why would it? It was utterly out of keeping with everything he knew of her.

This posthumous clue threw out of kilter the lustral narrative that had been collectively maturing over five weeks. He didn't know whether it made any difference, but had he been able to think clearly he might have realized that it was the ambiguous potential of it, as an answer to questions after the fact, that troubled him. He suspected it couldn't culminate in anything definitive and couldn't see how dissecting the nonsense, or following its shady trail, could yield a beneficial outcome. So what was the point? To cause more pain, to pose more questions?

He left the house, to get away from the idea, because despite all that there was an irrational allure to the possibility, still a desire to realize its role.

From late morning to early afternoon he occupied himself in the Tufnell Park Arms, reading the paper, having a pint or two, and playing pool with the barman. Trying to forget. It was deserted, as it always was on a weekday, and the barman was reticent and middle-aged. He knew Vic to see and he knew what he drank.

With Lali's death so recent, and so close, Vic assumed that the barman knew what had befallen him. It was possible, however, that he didn't. This was London after all. The barman certainly showed no signs of knowing, neither awkward nor sympathetic, barely speaking a word between shots and showing little interest in anything beyond the 2:15 at Crayford.

About half an hour before Jessica was due home, Vic left the pool table. The barman nodded and went back to work. Once home, Vic tidied up the living room and threw some dirty dishes into a sink of boiling, soapy water, to erode the encrusted leftovers. He thought Orla might feel the need to drop in.

When he opened the door to them, Orla indicated five minutes, her fingers and thumb fanned out and her palm pushed to the fore, while she carried on a phone call on the doorstep. Jessica rounded her waist and traipsed past him with a languid wave and a greeting of bored indifference, 'Hi, Dad,' as Orla pulled the door closed on herself. Jessica threw off her prodigally large and practically empty schoolbag – holding only a reader and two copies – with a turn of her left shoulder and a flick of her wrist and arm. The bag slid down her arm, into the momentary grip of her fist, before seamlessly skimming over the dolphined arc of her palm and fingers, as her wrist pivoted and released; an everyday ballet of velvety smoothness. The bag glided to its usual resting place beneath the hall table, crushed up against the dusty skirting.

He was still attempting to find out how her day had been when she took the stairs, two steps at a time. He called up to her to change out of her uniform. She shouted back at him, from her bedroom, where the uniform would be dumped on the floor and left to crumple in a heap, 'You don't need to tell me that every day, you know.'

'Yeah,' he said, as he sat down, eyes fixated on the web address on the bottom of the page. 'I do actually. And hang it properly.'

He heard Orla letting herself in and pushed the poem in among the unpaid bills on the kitchen table.

'I'm sorry about this morning,' she said, heading off any meaningless pleasantries. 'I shouldn't have said anything.'

'Don't worry about it,' he assured her.

Dinner was a rather bland, supermarket frozen cod, with broccoli and boiled, baby potatoes. He planned to get Jessica homeworked, fed, entertained, readied for bed and tucked up by eight-thirty in the evening. Then he wanted to find whatever there was to be found with regard to the verse from the grave and never have cause to consider it again.

'Daddy?' she half whined, and he knew they were in a negotiation.

'Yes, Jess?'

'What would you do if I weren't here?'

'Read in silence,' he replied.

'Is that what you did when Mum would be here?'

He felt the cavity of his chest when they discussed Lali. Dry pangs of repression. And Jessica's messy past-conditional 'would' made it all the worse. It placed Lali somewhere between extant and remembered. But he had resolved to allow any talk of Lali to go unchecked, and to answer questions about her as close to honestly as sound judgment permitted. This allowed for what felt like a perpetual dialogue on the subject. 'I suppose, yeah,' he said.

'Can I lie down here until I fall asleep?'

'It would only be news you'd be watching.'

'But I wouldn't even be watching. I just want to sleep here. With you.'

'I don't know, Jess. You'd sleep better in your own bed.'

'Please,' she whimpered.

His protest foundered. 'Okay, but you're not stretching out on the floor there, like a cat.'

He turned on the news as she jumped onto the couch. As she lay down, he tucked a couple of cushions under her head, wrapped a throw around her, tucking her in tight, toes to chin. He dropped back into his chair and took up his book, where the poem was folded between two pages, and read it for the hundredth time.

Around ten o'clock, he lifted her from the couch and carried her upstairs, still wrapped up like a pupal butterfly. She collapsed her head into his neck, her nose cold, but remained unawakened. He lowered her onto her bed and kissed her goodnight, before returning downstairs to lock up and turn off the TV.

In the office, he placed his glass of wine down and switched on the computer and the internet modem. He googled, *Murder for Me*. It threw back at him: JA Rule lyrics for Murder Me; Amazon. com: play Murder For Me, DVD – Vic Wagner and Megan Scoggins; Baretta – Murder for Me, TV.com. At that point he gave up scrolling down. He checked the internet history but it revealed nothing. So he went back to the printed page and prepared to type in the web address that had been staring him in the face, daringly, all evening. It was faintly printed, but it was there. At the bottom of the page, unapologetic. An electronic fingerprint.

It lead to DUST, an acronymous website: Depression, Unhappiness, and Suicide Together. He presumed DUST to be a forum for discussion, possibly a safe-haven of support and advice. Though even when he thought the site was as benign as that, it occurred to him that the acronym was symbolically morose and inappropriate, some kind of postmodern pastiche, half-clever and deliberately ill-defined; parody less the laughter.

There were links to chat-rooms and lists of literature related to the subject, information on legal issues surrounding suicide and assisted suicide. And most startling of all was the link to *Suicide Methods*. Once again, it was even worse than he imagined. He was expecting a list that named the different methods a person might consider: 1. Poison; 2. Hanging; 3. Slitting wrists. And even the thought of that caused him to blench. But this was a 358KB file, solely text, fifty-four pages long, detailing methods of suicide, required dosages, availability of drugs, time taken to reach the 'blissful, blackened silence,' availability of necessary substances and tools, a five-star rating system evaluating each method's likelihood of success, and addendums, notes advising on some of the pitfalls to be avoided.

There were details on how to 'self-deliver' with anything from cyanide and hydrogen to everyday products like bleach and caffeine. There was even the inimical suggestion of nitrous oxide – N20, laughing gas – accompanied by detailed notes, which included among them the suggestion that the local dentist's supply might be the most readily available. It explained the advantages of combining the gas with marijuana, for an absolutely painless demise, the probable cost, how to use a breathing mask, and the required dosage in the blood.

The listed methods ranged from the brutal to the inane: breaking your neck, including a body-weight/recommended-drop index; jumping off buildings – six storeys gives you a ninety percent chance of success, rising thereafter – and a cautionary note that an unsuccessful jump may leave you paralysed and unable to finish the job; asphyxiation; shooting yourself; decapitation, with a note referring you to the Jumping In Front Of Trains section; lethal plants and fungi; disembowelment; drowning; electrocution; starving to death; micromachines, dismissed as 'silly' in brackets, as were sucking your brains out and World War III; acid baths, 'available at most auto-repair shops and suiting those who enjoy extreme pain and don't want to leave a mess for others to clean up'; and then – AIDS.

Elsewhere, a selection of stolen lyrics from a diversity of songwriters, all celebrating or revering the 'final exit,' were presented like citations from the gospel of a cult – centered, enlarged, emboldened quotes, extracted and hung above the complete body of songs, as if they were seminal teachings of the faith, a gateway to a deathly nirvana. There were tracts of popular song lyrics: Metallica's *Fade to Black*, The Smiths's *Asleep*, the theme tune to M.A.S.H. – *Suicide Is Painless*.

It was the work of innumerable contributors, the tonal irregularity throughout the site a reminder of that. Some of it was presented earnestly, plainly informational, while other parts took on shades of travesty. The confusion served to make the whole site feel untrustworthy; it was unregulated, uncompassionate, informative yet misleading, unconventional and discomforting.

What was unexpected was how easily lured he was by the mercurial deceptions of DUST. He tore into it with the vanity of his own importance, with the naive belief that something could be achieved. He identified it as the focal point for his anger; at last, he had something to rage against.

He then attempted to enter one of its chatrooms. Entry was barred. Following the on-screen cues, he pounded heavy-fingered through the registration procedure, entering his email address and selecting a username – VIC13 – as well as a password. He waited impatiently over his email account for the confirmation of registration. Then he returned to DUST only to find a blank window where the chatroom was supposed to be. He slammed the keyboard down. As if in response to his indignation, a message popped up on the screen, informing him that he may need to adjust his browser settings and instructing him how to do it. Having done so, he entered and set upon the room's two users. He was literally trembling with hostility; a formless rage.

When he barged into that chatroom calling them miserable freaks and cowardly pricks, what he was looking for was confirmation. And confirmation needed no affiliation with truth. He wanted somebody, even one of those faceless vultures, to come clean and tell him that Lali had never loved him, that she'd confessed it before she filled her belly with over the counter drugs and vodka and swung herself from a beam. He wanted somebody to relay the facts of her confession to him, to tell him that she'd never wanted Jessica and that he had cajoled her into a life she resented. He wanted somebody to tell him it was all his fault. Because her memory threatened to ruin him, to reduce him to nothing, if he just let it be.

The discovery of the poem, and the interaction with the website, supplied his slowly shifting anger with manic acceleration.

And once it had begun, the feelings then came too fast and too hard. The terse control he had held over everything began to slip away on him.

He typed in *Murder for Me* into the website's search engine and let it do its work. Within seconds a link to the poem appeared and he clicked on it. Just as it had been on the printed page, there it was before him, except that on the screen it was offset against an ochre background. But it provided no more detail than what he already had; an anonymously posted few lines. He returned to the home page and followed the links to a listing of all the poems and stories posted on the site. He scrolled down through the titles, clicking on a few and reading several awful lines before moving to the next one.

He browsed the site for hours, reading submitted poetry and prose, painfully needy, though not unique. Poorly written stories, mostly, of lives that were simply unhappy. There were excerpts from famous literary figures like Poe and Plath, Dickinson, Tennyson, Blake and Byron. An entire world of dark thought, where people who already had dark thoughts came to visit, compounding it, and celebrating those who had left for a place from where no correspondence was possible.

Another piece of work that intimated the same sentiments or used the same imagery was what he was in search of, some stylistic signature that might lead him to somebody. But they were impossible to distinguish between. From the cringe worthy worst to the barely palatable best, it was merely mimicking the great melancholiers of the literary world, and often out-and-out plagiarizing; how many dug graves to let them lie or dreamed of endless nights?

Returning, in exasperation, to the chatrooms, he entered each one in turn, each with suitably grim epithets: Exit Eternity: Departure Rapture; Self-Deliverance; Hopeless; Quietus; Melancholy Heaven; Somnambulistic Joy; Final Countdown; and DUST2DUST. 'Is anyone here the author of *Murder for Me*? Or does anyone know Lali?' he asked, but received mostly nothing. There was the odd, 'I don't know,' and then a few hostiles encouraging him to leave the room if he was some kind of journo, or a grieving relative. It wasn't clear which was more abhorent. Late into the night, he chased and harassed and eventually threatened, but uncovered nothing.

Jessica's breath, dreamy and auroral, and pitched to the forefront of morning's unseeing silence, fluttered on his cheek and woke him. The sweetness of her breath hung in the air, uniquely and intangibly hers. It was eight o'clock and he was writhen on the couch, slack-jawed with tiredness, and encrusted with dried drool and gummy sleep, with the customary bottle of wine standing on the floor, beside the sofa.

Out of one eye, he looked up to the smiling but muddled Jessica; baby-faced, slender-limbed, inculpable.

'Dad, I think it's school time. I'm hungry.'

He had remained awake well into the morning, sitting despairingly before the computer, scouring the website for hours, until he was no longer able to see the screen or coordinate his typing. Then he went downstairs, awake but not much more. He opened another bottle, and went for it with intent, only to run out of steam and fall into the untroubled but dreamless sleep of a drunk. But awoken, with Jessica gone upstairs to dress and Orla's arrival imminent, he was eager to get Jessica ready and preserve a façade of functionality.

She had just set foot on the floor of the hallway when Orla could be heard beckoning her with a gentle squeak of her horn. He turned Jessica round and fastened her skirt. Then he dropped a slice of buttered toast onto some kitchen paper, stuck a small carton of juice into her hand, slipped the straps of her bag over her shoulders, and pushed her out the door with a hug and kiss. She raced toward the car, her merely decorative schoolbag bouncing erratically, toast clenched in one hand and juice in the other, as he waved to Orla from the porch. He indicated something about Jessica's hair and Orla held up a brush taken from the dash and rattled it, ever prepared.

He took a mug of coffee to the office and logged onto the DUST forum again, reading conversations, occasionally contributing. On and off throughout the day, users came and went with the changing circumstances in all the time zones beyond the interlinked hypertext. Hours passed, as the people behind the faceless usernames distinguished themselves from one another by their idiolects, foibles of expression, choices of phrase, attitudes, and even misspellings.

The enormity, the sheer global reach of it struck him. These people could be anywhere – North America, Asia, Scandinavia, Australia, Dublin, London, or as near as one door either side of him. Whoever he was looking for could have been in any backwater in the world and present themselves, in reality, nothing like their chatroom manifestation. If Lali had visited, the people she spoke with could have been just like him, there by mistake, and then never returned. Or just voyeuristic, curiously amusing themselves with the difficulties of others. They might be dead themselves. Or they mightn't have been there at all. They mightn't have been anywhere, existing only in Vic's deductive logic.

The endeavour began to feel hopeless. With all the alter-egos and allusive usernames, how could he be sure of anything? His blunt questions roused suspicion, made the impermanent identities back off. Or else they turned on him. He didn't speak the language. They picked him out immediately – an outsider. Just going there looking for answers marked him as suspect. They smelled him coming, a high-speed internet mile off.

Around midday, he dressed and left the house. He returned from the corner shop with a day's worth of booze and junk food, and a sliced pan. Supplied for the time being, he settled back down and honed in again on DUST. With eyes sore and hungover, he squinted at the computer screen. He gritted his teeth through his yawns and tried to swallow them down. More hours passed, but no progress. He persisted, watching and waiting.

In mid-afternoon, he phoned Orla and asked her if Jessica could stay the night with them. Orla was concerned but agreed. 'We've got her, Vic. There's no problem there. You get a night's rest. I'll drop her to school in the morning and swing by and pick you up. We'll go for a coffee or something. How about it?'

'Sure,' he said. 'Sure, yeah. School. Thanks.'

He cut into some bottles of beer. Walking up and down the stairs for each new bottle helped him stay awake through late afternoon and early evening. Occasionally, he had to slap himself sharply across the cheek to stay awake. By late evening he'd scaled the walls of tiredness and he began to feel unexpectedly fresh; a second wind.

He continued to roam from chatroom to chatroom, a mouse click here and there, with a volley of typed interjections every so often. Waiting for something but not knowing quite what, he grew impatient with the self-importance, the strained, uncomfortable yearning and the ludicrous yet obscene discussions, and their unabashed championing of the irreversible.

There were rooms discussing what was referred to as the *suicidal impulse*, and pseudo-academic exercises and excerpts from out of copyright texts, and various cultural perspectives on the act. Still more links brought him to lists and reviews of the best films or music related to the theme, even pinpointing key scenes and the precise minute in the movie or song where they appeared – a tortured scream, a textbook jump, a poetic slide from consciousness.

And then, back again, like a loop, to rooms that seemed like suicide anonymous, where users talked about how and when, about those who had made it, and those who failed; failure, and particular repeated failure, was received with disdain – 'If you're really serious, there's no need for failure.'

The site's uselessness gradually became apparent and he returned to the words, in exhaustion, and without the will to fight them. He read the poem and reread it. But the answer just wasn't there, no matter how often or closely he looked – screaming it out at the top of his voice, whispering it uncouthly, like a madman, to the bathroom mirror. He even sang the words to the tune of *Yellow Submarine*, commandeering the most inane tune he could think of and infusing it with the most pointless words he'd ever read.

As he read it back for the final time, he remembered her floating above the floor with the life squeezed out of her. He folded the page carefully and then tore it, left it down beside him on the desk and began flicking through some photos on the computer.

Lali took photos everywhere they went. Of Jessica, mainly, but also of Vic, and even of the two of them from time to time. And seascapes. And sunsets and sunrises – recurring motifs. The endings and beginnings of things. In retrospect, he realized that it had always been the more arduous middles that caused Lali greatest difficulty. The lack of the spectacular in them, the nuts and bolts of life. Her nature didn't easily lend itself to the mundane. It was always in pursuit of thrills and ecstasies, or crises.

After coming back up from the kitchen, he opened up the music library on the computer and flicked through some albums before selecting a random mix and turning back to the photos. He wanted to feel something as he looked at Lali on the screen, mostly smiling but sometimes frowning, and even sleeping.

Eventually he paused over one photo. She was almost the entirety of the screen. Her smooth skin was a shade darker than usual and her hair fell beautifully down one side of her face. In the peripheral spaces beyond the outline of her smiling head, the dusky colours of a Tuscan sky could be seen, sculpted around her, making her more beautiful even than she was, as she sat back into the green and white striped canvas of her deckchair. An image of happiness, away from it all for a week in Italy, on a good night where she was everything he imagined.

A happy memory. Except he couldn't remember the happiness. She smiled back at the camera, and although the image before him on the screen evoked memories of sensuous summer evenings, wine and bread, olives and dust, with Jessica table-side, in a booster chair, all he could remember of Lali was that she sat there opposite him. None of *her* survived. No essence of her remained. It was like he was looking at a girl in a brochure for Tuscan holidays, but nobody he knew.

He remembered how he used to threaten to have that photo enlarged and mounted in the living room – she hated any photograph of herself. But now there was nothing. He couldn't see Lali there at all. He couldn't remember what made her smile like that. Was that smile real? Did they ever enjoy each other that much? Or was she just the leech he remembered, incessantly dissatisfied. Somebody he didn't really know and who didn't really like him.

He looked away from the screen, confused by what he thought was a lack of emotion, but then suddenly turned back and glared at the image as if it was Lali herself, and shouted at her. She just continued to smile back, unmoved, and he spat at the screen – in her face – and stood up. He watched the splatter of spit pebble-dash the screen and the single phlegmy pellet slide down over her nose, and across her smiling mouth.

Downstairs, shortly after, he strode toward the knocking on the front door. It seemed intent on challenging him, seemed to want something from him. It was angry. So was he.

Donna, her hair a threadbare mess and her face afflictively reddened, stood in the porch. Her open hand was raised to crash down on the door once again when he opened it. She was upset, he could see, and she was drunk. She was probably on something powdery or pilled too, he thought. What she was upset about, he had no idea. A new hamster, perhaps, or the colour of the rain. Donna was always upset about something. The world was forever playing cruel games with her.

'I need to talk to you,' she said, forcing past him, walking down the hall and turning into the living room.

In the aftermath of Lali, he had been without the emotional resources to deal effectively with Donna. He recognized that she brought practical benefits – she knew Rococo's business well – and it seemed easiest to just leave her where she had always been, and so he did. While he pitied her, he hadn't disposed of her or demoted her. She was simply passed over, as he appointed Aldo instead as Rococo's manager.

He had some understanding of Donna's suffering and had tolerated her fits of maniacal blame, until then. Because he knew she was defenseless against Lali, even more so than he. But as she stood before him in their living room that evening, with the phrenetic cocktail of pained memory, sleep deprivation and alcohol, fizzing through him, his sole thought was for how Donna had always hated him. And he was tired of being hated.

'Donna, this isn't a good time,' he warned.

'What are you going to do with those ashes?' she asked, bluntly, looking toward the urn.

'I'll let you know.'

'If you do something without asking me, you'll be fucking sorry.'

'Donna,' he said, in a tone as threatening as he had ever uttered, 'you're going to be sorry if you don't get out of my house.'

'Your house! This is Lali's house, you wanker. You Irish fuck! You're only here because of Jessie. Give me the ashes! She'd have wanted me to have them.'

'She didn't know what she wanted.'

'Give her to me!'

'I'll give her to you, alright, the house as well, when you can guarantee me that I'll never have to look at your beaten mug again.'

'I want Rococo's. It was ours. It should be mine now. She'd have been fucking sick if she knew you were going to be running it. It's ours.'

'You're a paid hand, Donna. Remember that. I don't remember you injecting any cash or taking on any risk. You hear what I'm saying?'

'I've given everything to that place. I helped build it.'

'But it's not yours.'

'Fuck you! Lali would have wanted me to have it. Why would she give it to you?'

'She didn't,' he reminded her, with condescension and spite. 'And I really can't see the courts handing the management of her estate over to you, her junky friend. Now, get out!' They had inched closer to each other as they shouted, and came face to face, her leering upward to meet his aggression with her own.

'It's your fucking fault. Yours!' she cried. 'You pushed her to it.'

He quieted down. 'Donna, leave now. Last time of warning.'

'You fucking killed her! You! If you had . . . '

Everything that was wrong with what Donna was doing converged on him. What if Jessica had been home? After doing what he could to tolerate Donna, how did she think she was going to be allowed into their house and subject him to this? When she pushed herself past Vic, she couldn't have known it just wasn't the night for it.

'Out! You daft bitch!' he roared into her face, before grabbing her by both shoulders, turning and shoving her toward the door and into the hallway. She leaned back into him, trying to prevent him pushing her to the front door. He stooped down and slung his arm around her waist and reached over to the back of her head, and forced her forward again. All the time she was screaming abuse and threatening him – 'You killed her! Don't you fucking touch me!'

She faced him then, crouched down, like a wrestler. Her expression livid. Then she took another run at him from two or three paces. He didn't know what it was she was trying to achieve. Was it just to stay in the house, out of defiance? Or did she just want to beat him, to successfully challenge his authority over Lali's legacy, right there and then, in an all out catfight? He placed one foot back to steady himself for the impact and caught her in both arms, before shoving her back down the hallway. Her head jerked back and collided with a coat-hook, as he drove her into the back of the door. He pinned her there with his weight and one hand, while he undid the latch with his other, ready to open the door and fling her out. She screeched and winced as her head began to pound; a delayed pain. He manoeuvered her scratching and kicking body around the opening door, her pushing against him all the time, until finally it was opened wide enough for him to force her out. With one push, he sent her through the narrow porch. She stumbled backwards over the front step and ended up sprawled on the short garden path. 'I'd start my long job search if I was you!' he seethed down at her.

She sat up and was quiet, given up on the fight, and then started to cry. She tried to speak a few times, something angry; panting and hateful.

She was already beaten, but he persisted. 'Take a look at yourself, Donna. If you want somebody to blame. You're a mess! You're pathetic. What Lali needed were stronger voices, not fawning, needy retards. You indulged her! You're a mess, Donna. And what's worse, what I really don't get, is that she did this to you. She kicked you around, ruined you, and now that she's dead, you're still defending her. You're a mess, Donna. Go home!' He closed the door on her and locked it.

He was not yet capable of recognizing the man he'd become – a surly drunk, scrapping and abusing a woman on his doorstep, openly and uninhibited. Not yet able to line-up his old self beside the drunk, and see how far off-road he'd gone.

He paced the living room, necking a bottle of wine. He kicked a light, wooden side-table and sent it and the some old newspapers into the air, smashing an empty glass against the fireplace. He gulped down another massive mouthful and stood steady for several minutes. He turned on the stereo, cranking up the sound, almost as high as it could go, sure to disturb the neighbours, and played whatever happened to be in it.

He began walking the house, and noticing Lali's old address

book on the hall table, he tore it in half and threw its rough cuttings against the front door. As if the momentum of a dissolute rabble had been unleashed, he began picking up and tearing apart anything that was Lali's, or reminded of her, and flinging it about the place: a coat, a magazine, the mirror above the hall table – shattered and in splinters on the floor.

Out of breath, he paused. Then he strode out to the shed in the back garden. He smashed the flimsy bolt with a rock and flung the door open. He piled three cardboard boxes into each other and made for the house. An elderly neighbour was looking down on him from his second floor window as he stepped out of the shed. Vic gave him the two fingers and the man ducked behind his curtain.

Back in the house, he dropped the boxes to the floor in the hall and began filling one of them with the things he'd thrown about. Then he took another box, the coat having taken up most of the space in the first, into the living room, and began the cull.

The bookshelf was the most obvious place to start – if he could clear it of CDs and DVDs and magazines, and ornamental bloody camels, he could make use of it as it was intended, as a bookshelf. How she'd hate this if she's watching, he thought; *NME, Mojo, Kerrang! K Mag, American Pie, Trainspotting, Requiem for a Dream, 28 Days Later, Jackass, The Killing Fields, Leaving Las Vegas, Amelie, Waking the Dead, Crouching Tiger Hidden Dragon, The Godfather* – only Part III?, *Rear Window, Cinema Paradiso, Happiness*, Leonard Cohen, Sandy Shaw, The Libertines, Nick Cave, John Martyn, The Stone Roses, Abba, Macy Gray, Nina Simone, Tom Waits, and a whole host of Drum & Base rubbish, and dance music that he didn't recognize or care for, were among the titles never seen again.

Then he topped the spiteful pile with two Kilim cushions he'd always hated. Some counterfeit sneak had sold them to her out of the back of a jeep, in Ankara, on the holiday taken shortly after they moved to Huddleston Road. The man had passed them off as precious amulets, woven by a Turkish seamstress. He looked at Lali, just beginning to show, and told her that the patterns were 'the wolf's mouth.' The turquoise wolf's mouth appearing like conjoined packmen, back to back, with a serrated outline, against a red background, with shafts of yellow sewn in at intervals; supernatural protection for her and her family. She always said she knew it was bollocks; loudly, she said it, but not with quite enough surety. That kind of ethnic novelty had always reeled her in, which was odd, given her usually reliable scepticism. Vic had always put it down to the mystical unknowns of her errant father; that desperate need for some connection to the fraud.

As a consequence of this weakness, the house had been littered with mass-produced, vastly over-priced ornaments, masks, Phad-like paintings, clumsy lumps of wood sculpture and shit pottery. Some of it made it onto shelves or walls, but most of it ended up stuffed into rarely opened drawers; the magic invariably wore off once it entered the walls of westernized suburbia. Except for the cushions.

The cushions lasted. She curled up with her head on them every night and wrapped her arms around them as if they were all that could save her. He used to tease her: 'Chances are that the Turk in the Jeep hails from Kingsland Road and calls himself Peter in the off-season.' She hated that, like Vic hated the cushions, with their mock ethnicity, their hocus pocus.

Slung in the cradle of his arms were the three cardboard boxes. Stacked one on top of the other. He carried them to the bottom of the road with a deceptive appearance of purpose. At the junction with Tufnell Park Road he stood before a skip. Her memories and miscellaneous belongings were then shot-putted into the air; the underside of each box balancing on the palm of his hand before being launched in a trembling push toward the summit of the heaped skip. Most of the contents scattered over the top of the mound already there – rusted pipework, a stained old toilet bowl, some pungent carpet – but a few stray CDs, and a magazine, fell, littering the road. He ignored them, other than to propel a CD cover crashing against the side of the skip with a swipe of his foot.

After the tussle with Donna the potency of the unsaid had been lost. The altercation had freed him from the social protocol of bereavement. All the feckless words he'd kept to himself, encased beneath the spongy shutter of his tongue, as it strained to speak but got thwarted by propriety, now began to find projection.

You can't, but he wanted to erupt every time some acquaintance of Lali's that he'd never previously met offered their condolences through the words, 'The poor woman,' or a similar sentiment. Screw her, he thought. What about them, him and Jessica? Topping herself was nothing more than the final, and greatest, act of selfishness that Lali ever committed. Poor nothing! She didn't get what she deserved, but she got what she asked for. So, good enough for her, that's what he thought.

With the unthinkable having been thought, and no longer braced by restraint, he began to feel disarmed. He closed the door and made his way to the living room. He swept down open-clawed for the bottle of wine. The music continued to bleat and blare, pushing the speakers beyond their capacity, virtually to explosion. He sat down, the wine bottle gripped by the neck. He glared ahead of him and just remembered her; how she might have sat there once. He wondered what it was she thought, all those nights they spent in that room.

He drank more wine and then opened another bottle. He walked around the house, from room to room. In the kitchen, the music from the living room flooded the floor. He watched his reflection swaying in the window. His head swam. Hunger clenched; but he didn't want to eat. More punishment.

Eventually the loud music began to irritate him and he pulled the plug on the stereo and phoned home.

'Vic, how are you? Is everything okay?' his mother enquired.

'Fine. It's good now. You're good people, you know.'

'Vic?'

'Always been good people. How do you get to find good people?'

'Vic, what's the matter? I'll get your father.'

'Mum, there's no need . . . '

In the interlude between his mother and father's changeover, he lost his train of thought.

'Vic, is everything okay? Is Jessie okay?' his father asked.

'She's fine, Dad. Best of hands, the best of hands.'

'Where is she, Vic? Jessie, where is she?'

'Orla's got her.'

'Good. That's good. What can I help you with then, son?'

'I'm glad that . . . you're good people. A strong man. That's you. Mum, and Mum. Good people. How do good people find each other, Dad? That's the question of our time.'

'Vic, I want you to listen to me now. You need to get yourself to sleep. And ring us in the morning.'

'No! No, no, Dad!'

'Vic, you need sleep. You're shit-faced, son.'

'Dad, no. Listen. You guys, and Jessie, you're . . . I love you.'

After that, the phone went down and Vic returned to the small office with the fury of earlier spent. Even when he looked around and saw all the traces of Lali that had escaped the culling – more magazines, CDs, and bric-a-brac – he was not moved to deal with them. Half an hour before he might have thrown them out the window.

He dropped onto the chair in front of the computer. The family photographs were still on a loop. Photo after photo faded in then out. Familiar faces and occasions. But they stood apart from him. Precious but painful, and yet there was a farness too.

A few more minutes passed before he turned up the volume on the computer's speakers. Their musical history was also on a loop, the soundtrack to the photo slideshow. Randomly, the computer shuffled through albums – his, hers, theirs. Then came the opening seconds – a gentle introductory roll of drum, the tinkle of keyboards, and then the gravelly lament, almost like a voice breaking into manhood from squeaky adolescence, but deeper;

a trembling voice, close to defeat. The gritty vocal poured over the top and sifted through the layers of music, underscoring its bittersweet flavor, and the steady bass that plucked away beneath it all, virtually unheard, was a neat, reliable rhythm to hang the cathartic devastation on – *Sweet Little Mystery*.

Tears. He put his face in his hands, hiding the grief for fear she was still watching, somehow. He shuddered from his coccyx; a chill from the core. Intending to steel himself, he reached out for a drink. But he was disorientated. The bottle neck was greasy in his palm and slipped from his grasp. He tried to stabilize himself upon the desk as the bottle thudded downward and its contents gulped out. His knees were long gone and the rubbery freefall was inching upward into his chest. Into the mind. His searching hand scuffed the side of the cheap, self-assembled desk, his skin frictionless on the surface, and his strength diminished to nothing. He lurched forward. He tumbled sideways out of the chair as the dead weight he'd become followed his hand to the floor. After hitting it, taking the seat toppling over with him and kicking the sliding keyboard into the air, he scrambled from the wreckage. He stared at the fallen chair, and up to the speakers and screen, from the nearest wall. His knees were pulled to his chest and the leg of his trousers and his T-shirt were stained by the pool of wine he'd collapsed onto. To his surprise, the tears were still streaming; heavy, soundless, man tears. There was none of the emotional extrication that usually accompanies tearfulness, just a tumescent wetness of the eyes. He could have stood up, among his family, had he had the strength, and told them nothing was wrong, for all he felt of it, as they looked back at him and told him in disbelief, 'But you're covered in tears.' He felt fine. He felt nothing. He felt everything.

The song had caught him out, passed surreptitiously through his skin and muscle fibre and bone, and lanced him. There was the desolation that she identified with, that was inherent, and that he only then discovered despite years of listening and making appreciative noises. All of a sudden the sound was new. It meant something more. He felt close to her. His heart was in his feet somewhere, fallen with the wrinkled weight of a half-filled water balloon. He didn't know what he felt, really, until it crossed his chest again. Hyperventilating, he tipped himself over and lay on the floor. He was aware of every tear as they cut transversal tracks across his face. He gaped up and sideways at the pictures of Lali – for she was all he could see out of the corner of his eye, as she appeared, then faded, only to reappear. Over and over, a life from which he would never disentangle himself, on an endless whorl.

He couldn't have been lying on the floor for any more than a matter of hours, when he heard Orla's voice carrying above him. But he couldn't respond. Then he felt her arm around him.

She took him to be drunk, or *just* drunk. Despite being incapable of speech, he succeeded in walking with her to her car, guided and held upright. He heard her on the phone talking with Geoff, calmly informing him of their imminent arrival and quickly assessing the situation between them – accounting for Vic, Jessica, and considering how to bring him under their care with the least conspicuousness. And yet, later, although he could hear her voice, he could discern almost nothing of her words.

In the days that followed, he could only recall vague images and snippets of conversations that had proceeded above his head, or aside from him. But he mistrusted them in the aftermath, dismissing them as mere hotchpotch observations, made somewhere below the conscious, as Orla brought him to his feet.

Geoff had met them and guided him from Orla's car. He showed Vic down the hall, through the kitchen, down the three steps, under the low arch, and left Vic sitting dazed on the bed.

As he sat there, his eyes stretched wide with chronic insomnia and his weightless stare travelling absently across the room, his mind began to weave an indiscriminate path through memory, fantasy and illusion. Tears streamed from his face again as he found an abstract memory of Lali standing before him, only kinder than he'd ever known her. She was unrecognizably at ease. He remembered her back in Tuscany, on the terrace, with the free-standing stone farmhouse, shielded on each side by a row of quintessential Cypress trees – pointed, ancient, superstitious. She looked out over the vineyard as it fell away below the farmhouse, like furrowed tracks down the hillside, toward the small olive grove at the foot of the hill, and he thought then of a different life they might have lived, in rural Italy. Imagined himself talking to tourists about grapes and the decision that saved their lives. And for a moment he was alone, watching the soil sift through his fingers in dusty clumps.

But into the idyllic illusion crept doubt. He tilted his head slightly and looked across the room, as though Lali was really there, remembering something close to reality, before it merged with something less than real but more than fabrication; an al fresco dining space opened up like a yawning chasm between them, and a contemptuous silence throbbed in the air. But then memories of how they used look lovingly at Jessica, and catch each other doing so, brought a faint smile. He imagined Jessica dancing from foot to foot against the streaky Tuscan backdrop; the taut lines of orange and red and yellow behind her, plumped up by puffy strands of white and pink cloud, and the pitch-black profile of the hills on the far side of the valley, rippling and protruding into the evening azure. Her jester's dance mocked the otiose stoicism of the single tree that stood on the lucent skyline behind her – trimmed and erect, hard, deciduous, and resilient – and as his cheek sunk into the cool pillow, he slid seamlessly into a restorative coma.

* * *

Some fourteen hours later, with the vernal sun brightening the room, he awoke. He was flat on his back, and the perfectly folded sheets, tucked in under his armpits and moulded across his chest, were swaddling him in quietude. Small particles of dust held in the sunlit air, or rode gently on invisible currents, and settled on the still surface of water in a glass on the bedside locker.

From the kitchen he heard a radio projecting sensible BBC accents through the house, ricocheting from wall to ceiling to floor and into the spare room. He felt weak but alert as he lay still, flitting his eyes about the room, trying to orient himself.

He drifted dopily for an indefinite period of time before he rose and dressed in the clothes left out for him. Entering the immaculate kitchen, crumbless, unsmudged surfaces gleamed proudly, but without the suggestion of a house that daren't be touched by visiting hands and feet. There was a clemency to Orla's compulsive order.

The marble breakfast bar presented an as of yet unfilled teapot, three tea bags already dropped inside, and a woven basket of fresh bread. The warm, doughy aroma tickled at the bridge of his nose, and he lifted the glass lid from the butter dish. He buttered a small slice of bread and put his hand to the side of the kettle. It was warm and came quickly to the boil.

He assumed Jessica had been brought to school. But it surprised him that there was no sign of Orla. He expected her to greet him, to fill him in on the ugly details of his collapse and to be central to any resolution of his difficulties.

As he poured himself a mug of tea, turning the thoughtfully left newspaper to the sports pages, beginning just then to feel he had a handle on the morning, he noticed Orla. Through the French doors, and past some large potted plants on the raised patio, he saw her in the garden below. She was sitting with a mug of coffee and her writing pad.

He passed with hangdog tentativeness through the French doors, crossing the sandstone patio and descending the steps. With a side-plate of buttered fresh bread and a mug of tea, he took a seat across from Orla.

Although it was too soon, that morning, for scrutiny and questions of why and what exactly happened, it could hardly have been ignored completely, so he engaged.

'Did I call you last night?' he asked.

'No. Your parents rang,' she replied.

'Oh.'

'You told them you loved them. They were worried.'

'I don't remember. Not really.'

'I'm not surprised,' she said, looking up from her notepad.

She asked nothing more intrusive than how he was feeling. She was content to leave all that had happened to ferment. He still felt dazed as they spoke, but calm too. Orla scribbled notes and ran her red editing pen across the first draft of a chapter, as he savoured the warmth of his tea and lolled in the suburban sounds of the leafy garden. He talked a little, but mostly he just sat comfortably in her company.

The following weeks found them in many conversations that looked backward, in search of something they knew could never be more than indefinite. They tried to make sense of what happened – over coffee, on the phone, in her car. In the end, he came to accept that there was no sense to be made of the events surrounding Lali's final months. To accept his powerlessness.

'Sometimes it just overwhelms me,' he told Orla. 'The whole thing. The experience. All the contradictions.'

He could see that for those who had known Lali only in passing, that her final act would have seemed somehow incoherent, or illogical. But he had seen her standing on their doorstep on a winter's morning, with the cold thick on the windscreens, in her slippers and dressing gown. He remembered creeping quietly up on her, and hearing her, as the dark winter sky began to turn a hypothermic violet, still just before sunrise, with an almost full moon held low above the roof tops and the spindly crowns of the sycamores, as a few stars still glistened mistily in the iced air. He remembered her being startled by his arm slipped round her waist, and the kiss on the back of her neck, as his other hand swung a mug of coffee under her nose. And how she flinched, shrinking away from his touch, and glanced around, removing one earphone and drying her eyes quickly on her sleeve.

The memory of her, staring out at that stillness, with the gritty thrum of early traffic on Tufnell Park Road inaudible to her as the passively melodic, *Fuck This Shit*, played in her ears, waiting for yet another kind of sunrise, seemed a picture of vulnerability at the time. But in hindsight, it came to feel more like a sinister augur; it was often the most beautiful things that saddened her. Whenever he thought of it, he couldn't help but acknowledge that her fate had been coming from a long way out; an inner poison pollinated in her soul, flowering like her own lethal beauty.

While a part of him, he knew, would always play the victim to Lali, there was a vestigial sense of having failed her too. This ambivalence was the consequence of doubting the veracity of his own recollections, and appreciating their bias. It seemed more unlikely as the days passed, his story of a manipulative siren possessing power enough to turn him against his very self. It began to sound fanciful, and more like his own instability, as time wound on and he began to speak the words aloud. This made him fear for how it would sound in years, in decades time. The temptation then was to sit on the fence, not to utter the terrible thoughts he held.

His memory was sure to embellish one way or the other. It would never be accurate, so his discussions with Orla, and the scribblings in his journal, the stated record of his time with Lali, served as a remedy to revisionism and obituary-like histories; an antidote to memory. He confessed his feelings in all their luridness, and distinctly in their present. He didn't want to be accused of denigrating Lali when she wasn't around to defend herself, but neither did he want to have his recollections muddied by time, through his own nostalgia or that of others. He sought an interpretation of events that would stand.

'Lali's was a world of temporary transactions. People came and went, were useful or not, but held no importance to her other than in the moment,' he wrote. An emotional capitalist, he came to refer to her as, as likely to throw wads of affection your way as dump you when your share-value dipped. But her free-market principles were short-sighted, and she paid for them in the end, he supposed.

She was alienated too, of course, and disengaged, especially in the final months. He could see that, eventually, though he couldn't muster much sympathy; for he was one of the expendable commodities that she bought and sold. And sold and sold and sold. She sank into a kind of torpor, no longer able to attain pleasure from living. 'And then she just gave up,' he would say, flippantly, on days when he was tired of remembering.

But the speculative cost of remembering was never entirely borne. On the far side of that submissive conclusion, energies were replenished and further unknowns were scoured in search of Lali. How did it start? When had it started?

He wondered whether the thought had entered her head one day and then just never left; hung around waiting while everything she enjoyed ran its course, and then went to work on her.

Or was it more corrosive than that, an impulse whose pernicious influence ate away at her until she fell? Or an impulsive act, perhaps, a figurative hurling of herself down the stairs, in a moment of madness, a moment of disconnection from both her external reality and her psychological processes?

There were just too many inconsistencies and coincidences to know. Women didn't hang themselves, it was claimed. And the cable that did for her? Where had it come from? Had it just been lying around the house, unfortuitously discovered? Or had she gone out and actually bought it for purpose? And that beam. They had uncovered it a couple of years after moving in, when some cracked plaster fell from the ceiling. Lali insisted they uncover it. 'What am I to make of that project now?' he asked.

And then the poem too.

It was all too loaded with incertitude. Lali's life vehemently resisted conclusion. Remebering her was an ongoing, creative act, where she soon became something mythical, enhanced, diminished, re-imagined and abridged. That was how her infelicitous departure had rendered her. It was too long, the rest of his life, for a credible memory of her to have any hope of surviving.

All he had, really, in the end, was a litany of circumstantial and random happenings to consider as proof, which inevitably led him to the crux of the matter – himself. The only remaining subject of relevance, in the context of Lali's death.

Perhaps he had let her down. He was reluctant to say it, that she had been ill, because of the implications: when her riotous impetuousity took control of her, the culmination of months, years and decades of denial on the one hand, and ingrained despair on the other, what might he have done? When she had nothing to steady her and that inner discipline had failed, who could she have hoped to rely on?

And where had he been? How had he missed it?

And specifically that week, what critical signals had eluded him? These were the questions he was powerless in the face of. But then he asked himself, did he have a responsibility, really, given that she had forced *him* out? Wasn't that her final act?

Action, it has been said, is life, the opposite of thought and death. Hadn't she already begun to die? When she stopped fighting? As she tiredly acceded, and surrendered? Before he ever left? Wasn't she finished long before she stopped breathing?

So she remained among them. From the urn on the mantelpiece to tiny inconsequentials like Jessica's pink Converse, kicked off by the fireplace in exactly the fashion of her mother; falling against each other, one turned over with its toe to the heel of the other, and laces still tied, abandoned in the midst of some random fancy, the subtle disorder oddly endearing, natural and human against the perfect lines of the floorboards, as they ran fast and neat across the room.

Or she could be found, physically, in the posture of Jessica, sitting before the stereo, rooting through what remained of her mother's old CDs, pausing for longer periods on ones that caught her attention. As she routinely stumbled across songs whose qualities were potent and associative, Lali's memory would weep uncontrollably; Jessica pausing on them for sixty seconds or more. It would compel him to glance up from his book, and surprised each time by their effect, he would be unable to look away for as long as the song played; her crossed legs, the dark hair rippling down her back, the concentration. And it would be something good he would be remembering, but it was always tinctured with grief.

'I just hope she doesn't uncover that John Martyn album anytime soon,' Orla joked, as they sat up talking on the phone.

'I think I'm safe there. I believe that one went into the skip.'

Orla joked that he might think about deleting the song from the PC too, to ensure Jessica wouldn't spring it on him unexpectedly. He considered that but never acted on it, unsure whether it would have been an act of practicality or denial.

And then sometimes he brought Lali on himself. Googling her, discovering her reborn, reincarnated to be precise, in Saini Sunpura, a village in northern India. He found her being worshipped as a goddess for the misfortune of a condition known as craniofacial duplication – boasting one head and two faces. The act of Googling undermined any claims of happenstance, but even with that concession, what were the chances? Baby Lali, a two-faced anomaly mistaken for a deity. An uncanny metaphor extended to him by a fluke of molecular biology and timing.

But he learned no more about his Lali. There was nothing concrete out there that could ever be known about another person. So all he could do was come to terms with Lali's life, embrace her likeness as beheld in Jessica, because her death was beyond him.

Over time, he found that her absence occasionally passed through him without bitterness. And he was grateful. It meant that he didn't spoil Jessica's memories, and she could expand into life, unimpeded by hard knocks and disappointment. And who could say, he thought, maybe it would be Jessica who would come closest to understanding what happened Lali. One could be seen in the other, after all, which made one question more difficult than all the rest.

'Do you still love Mum?' she asked.

She waited, then, attentively, and as undaunted as if she had asked him whether he liked soup or not. 'It's complicated,' he responded, a word she had come to view as synonymous with dishonesty.

'Ahhh, Dad!' she exclaimed, before clasping her hands on her hips and frowning at him. 'Yes or no?'

'If I had to say . . . yes,' he conceded, rather glumly. Glumly because it was in fact the truth, although he knew it would have been so much easier if it wasn't. The calm – the truth – that came of his capitulation was this fact. Being unable to rid himself of Lali, of his memory of wanting so much for her to be happy with him, or of her phantom visitations – dreams of her draped naked across him in the dark – made moving on a process of perpetual labour. Lali was always there, in the contours of Jessica's gait, and he expected that he would never stop loving her; each time the pendulum reached the height of its arc on one side – bitterness and anger – it began its descent, again, through the cool of indifference, and rose with the pendular weight of ambivalent momentum to the height of its opposite – love gone but remembered.

Maybe time would put a cure to the troubling inconstancy, he sometimes allowed himself to believe. Because he needed to. Because love was the worst of what she left behind – an ambiguous legacy, forever subject to mutation. And one day, he thought, with a strange reluctance, he would find that she had been air-brushed beyond recognition, drained of all her erratic colour. 'She'll be beautiful and painless again, like before I really knew her,' he said. Purely aesthetic. Nothing but symmetry; a shoulder turned to a lens, a kink of fringe upon an angular, pursing face.

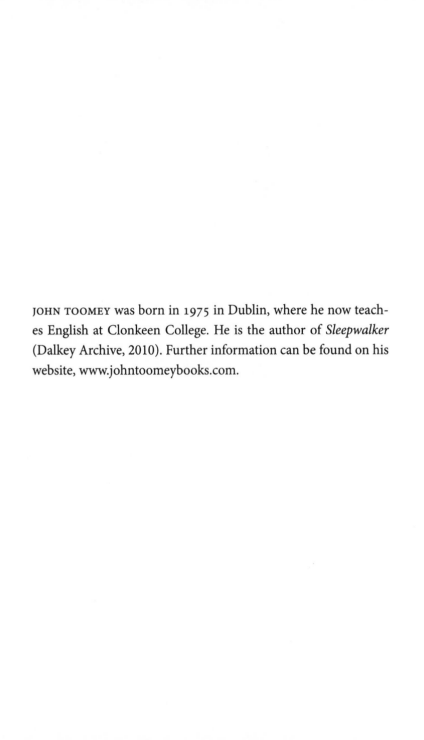

JOHN TOOMEY was born in 1975 in Dublin, where he now teach-
es English at Clonkeen College. He is the author of *Sleepwalker*
(Dalkey Archive, 2010). Further information can be found on his
website, www.johntoomeybooks.com.

ROSA LIKSOM, *Dark Paradise.*
OSMAN LINS, *Avalovara.*
   The Queen of the Prisons of Greece.
ALF MAC LOCHLAINN,
   The Corpus in the Library.
   Out of Focus.
RON LOEWINSOHN, *Magnetic Field(s).*
MINA LOY, *Stories and Essays of Mina Loy.*
BRIGITTE LOZEREC'H, *Sisters.*
BRIAN LYNCH, *The Winner of Sorrow.*
D. KEITH MANO, *Take Five.*
MICHELINE AHARONIAN MARCOM,
   The Mirror in the Well.
BEN MARCUS,
   The Age of Wire and String.
WALLACE MARKFIELD,
   Teitlebaum's Window.
   To an Early Grave.
DAVID MARKSON, *Reader's Block.*
   Springer's Progress.
   Wittgenstein's Mistress.
CAROLE MASO, *AVA.*
LADISLAV MATEJKA AND KRYSTYNA
   POMORSKA, EDS.,
   Readings in Russian Poetics:
     Formalist and Structuralist Views.
HARRY MATHEWS,
   The Case of the Persevering Maltese:
     Collected Essays.
   Cigarettes.
   The Conversions.
   The Human Country: New and
     Collected Stories.
   The Journalist.
   My Life in CIA.
   Singular Pleasures.
   The Sinking of the Odradek
     Stadium.
   Tlooth.
   20 Lines a Day.
JOSEPH MCELROY,
   Night Soul and Other Stories.
THOMAS MCGONIGLE,
   Going to Patchogue.
ROBERT L. MCLAUGHLIN, ED., *Innovations:*
   An Anthology of Modern &
   Contemporary Fiction.
ABDELWAHAB MEDDEB, *Talismano.*
GERHARD MEIER, *Isle of the Dead.*
HERMAN MELVILLE, *The Confidence-Man.*
AMANDA MICHALOPOULOU, *I'd Like.*
STEVEN MILLHAUSER, *The Barnum Museum.*
   In the Penny Arcade.
RALPH J. MILLS, JR., *Essays on Poetry.*
MOMUS, *The Book of Jokes.*
CHRISTINE MONTALBETTI, *The Origin of Man.*
   Western.
OLIVE MOORE, *Spleen.*
NICHOLAS MOSLEY, *Accident.*
   Assassins.
   Catastrophe Practice.
   Children of Darkness and Light.
   Experience and Religion.
   A Garden of Trees.
   God's Hazard.
   The Hesperides Tree.
   Hopeful Monsters.
   Imago Bird.
   Impossible Object.
   Inventing God.
   Judith.

   Look at the Dark.
   Natalie Natalia.
   Paradoxes of Peace.
   Serpent.
   Time at War.
   The Uses of Slime Mould:
     Essays of Four Decades.
WARREN MOTTE,
   Fables of the Novel: French Fiction
     since 1990.
   Fiction Now: The French Novel in
     the 21st Century.
   Oulipo: A Primer of Potential
     Literature.
GERALD MURNANE, *Barley Patch.*
   Inland.
YVES NAVARRE, *Our Share of Time.*
   Sweet Tooth.
DOROTHY NELSON, *In Night's City.*
   Tar and Feathers.
ESHKOL NEVO, *Homesick.*
WILFRIDO D. NOLLEDO, *But for the Lovers.*
BORIS A. NOVAK, *The Master of Insomia:*
   Selected Poems.
FLANN O'BRIEN, *At Swim-Two-Birds.*
   At War.
   The Best of Myles.
   The Dalkey Archive.
   Further Cuttings.
   The Hard Life.
   The Poor Mouth.
   The Third Policeman.
CLAUDE OLLIER, *The Mise-en-Scène.*
   Wert and the Life Without End.
GIOVANNI ORELLI, *Walaschek's Dream.*
PATRIK OUŘEDNÍK, *Europeana.*
   The Opportune Moment, 1855.
BORIS PAHOR, *Necropolis.*
FERNANDO DEL PASO, *News from the Empire.*
   Palinuro of Mexico.
ROBERT PINGET, *The Inquisitory.*
   Mahu or The Material.
   Trio.
A. G. PORTA, *The No World Concerto.*
MANUEL PUIG, *Betrayed by Rita Hayworth.*
   The Buenos Aires Affair.
   Heartbreak Tango.
RAYMOND QUENEAU, *The Last Days.*
   Odile.
   Pierrot Mon Ami.
   Saint Glinglin.
ANN QUIN, *Berg.*
   Passages.
   Three.
   Tripticks.
ISHMAEL REED, *The Free-Lance Pallbearers.*
   The Last Days of Louisiana Red.
   Ishmael Reed: The Plays.
   Juice!
   Reckless Eyeballing.
   The Terrible Threes.
   The Terrible Twos.
   Yellow Back Radio Broke-Down.
JASIA REICHARDT, *15 Journeys Warsaw*
   to London.
NOËLLE REVAZ, *With the Animals.*
JOÃO UBALDO RIBEIRO, *House of the*
   Fortunate Buddhas.
JEAN RICARDOU, *Place Names.*
RAINER MARIA RILKE, *The Notebooks of*
   Malte Laurids Brigge.

JULIÁN RÍOS, *The House of Ulysses.*
Larva: A Midsummer Night's Babel.
Poundemonium.
Procession of Shadows.
AUGUSTO ROA BASTOS, *I the Supreme.*
ALAIN ROBBE-GRILLET, *Project for a*
Revolution in New York.
DANIËL ROBBERECHTS, *Arriving in Avignon.*
JEAN ROLIN, *The Explosion of the*
Radiator Hose.
OLIVIER ROLIN, *Hotel Crystal.*
ALIX CLEO ROUBAUD, *Alix's Journal.*
JACQUES ROUBAUD, *The Form of a*
City Changes Faster, Alas, Than
the Human Heart.
The Great Fire of London.
Hortense in Exile.
Hortense Is Abducted.
The Loop.
Mathematics:
The Plurality of Worlds of Lewis.

The Princess Hoppy.
Some Thing Black.
LEON S. ROUDIEZ, *French Fiction Revisited.*
RAYMOND ROUSSEL, *Impressions of Africa.*
VEDRANA RUDAN, *Night.*
STIG SÆTERBAKKEN, *Self-Control.*
Siamese.
LYDIE SALVAYRE, *The Company of Ghosts.*
Everyday Life.
The Lecture.
Portrait of the Writer as a
Domesticated Animal.
The Power of Flies.
LUIS RAFAEL SÁNCHEZ,
Macho Camacho's Beat.
SEVERO SARDUY, *Cobra & Maitreya.*
NATHALIE SARRAUTE,
Do You Hear Them?
Martereau.
The Planetarium.
ARNO SCHMIDT, *Collected Novellas.*
Collected Stories.
Nobodaddy's Children.
Two Novels.
ASAF SCHURR, *Motti.*
CHRISTINE SCHUTT, *Nightwork.*
GAIL SCOTT, *My Paris.*
DAMION SEARLS, *What We Were Doing*
and Where We Were Going.
JUNE AKERS SEESE,
Is This What Other Women Feel Too?
What Waiting Really Means.
BERNARD SHARE, *Inish.*
Transit.
AURELIE SHEEHAN, *Jack Kerouac Is Pregnant.*
VIKTOR SHKLOVSKY, *Bowstring.*
A Hunt for Optimism.
Knight's Move.
A Sentimental Journey:
Memoirs 1917–1922.
Energy of Delusion: A Book on Plot.
Literature and Cinematography.
Theory of Prose.
Third Factory.
Zoo, or Letters Not about Love.
CLAUDE SIMON, *The Invitation.*
PIERRE SINIAC, *The Collaborators.*
KJERSTI A. SKOMSVOLD, *The Faster I Walk,*
the Smaller I Am.

JOSEF ŠKVORECKÝ, *The Engineer of*
Human Souls.
GILBERT SORRENTINO,
Aberration of Starlight.
Blue Pastoral.
Crystal Vision.
Imaginative Qualities of Actual
Things.
Mulligan Stew.
Pack of Lies.
Red the Fiend.
The Sky Changes.
Something Said.
Splendide-Hôtel.
Steelwork.
Under the Shadow.
W. M. SPACKMAN, *The Complete Fiction.*
ANDRZEJ STASIUK, *Dukla.*
Fado.
GERTRUDE STEIN, *Lucy Church Amiably.*
The Making of Americans.
A Novel of Thank You.
LARS SVENDSEN, *A Philosophy of Evil.*
PIOTR SZEWC, *Annihilation.*
GONÇALO M. TAVARES, *Jerusalem.*

Joseph Walser's Machine.
Learning to Pray in the Age of
Technique.
LUCIAN DAN TEODOROVICI,
Our Circus Presents . . .
NIKANOR TERATOLOGEN, *Assisted Living.*
STEFAN THEMERSON, *Hobson's Island.*
The Mystery of the Sardine.
Tom Harris.
TAEKO TOMIOKA, *Building Waves.*
JOHN TOOMEY, *Huddleston Road.*
Sleepwalker.
JEAN-PHILIPPE TOUSSAINT, *The Bathroom.*
Camera.
Monsieur.
Reticence.
Running Away.
Self-Portrait Abroad.
Television.
The Truth about Marie.
DUMITRU TSEPENEAG, *Hotel Europa.*
The Necessary Marriage.
Pigeon Post.
Vain Art of the Fugue.
ESTHER TUSQUETS, *Stranded.*
DUBRAVKA UGRESIC, *Lend Me Your Character.*
Thank You for Not Reading.
TOR ULVEN, *Replacement.*
MATI UNT, *Brecht at Night.*
Diary of a Blood Donor.
Things in the Night.
ÁLVARO URIBE AND OLIVIA SEARS, EDS.,
Best of Contemporary Mexican Fiction.
ELOY URROZ, *Friction.*
The Obstacles.
LUISA VALENZUELA, *Dark Desires and*
the Others.
He Who Searches.
MARJA-LIISA VARTIO, *The Parson's Widow.*
PAUL VERHAEGHEN, *Omega Minor.*
AGLAJA VETERANYI, *Why the Child Is*
Cooking in the Polenta.
BORIS VIAN, *Heartsnatcher.*
LLORENÇ VILLALONGA, *The Dolls' Room.*
TOOMAS VINT, *An Unending Landscape.*

FOR A FULL LIST OF PUBLICATIONS, VISIT:
www.dalkeyarchive.com